Dominic cleared his throat.

"I'll let Bailey know what we've discussed. She'll contact Rachel and ask her to draw up a new contract outlining the terms. Unless you'd prefer to initiate things?"

"No, that's fine. But I do have one more thing to ask."

"Name it."

Her lashes rose and resoluteness filled her expression. "This alliance is strictly professional. Our past doesn't factor into it. So there's no need to talk about Coral Cove."

"That's fine with me. As a rule, I don't talk about my private life with other people."

"I don't just mean we won't discuss Coral Cove with other people. We won't talk about it with each other. Ever."

He'd gotten what he'd wanted—a solution that kept his image intact, took care of everyone who depended on him and was also fair to Philippa.

But it didn't feel like a win. Avoiding their past or pretending it never existed felt like a betrayal of what they'd meant to each other six years ago.

But it was only a betrayal to him, wasn't it? Philippa hadn't felt the same way about their relationship. And he needed to accept that.

Taking physical steps away from Philippa and mental ones from their past, Dominic walked to the dresser for his phone. "If that's what you want, that's fine with me. I'll text Bailey now. You'll have a new contract by tomorrow."

Dear Reader,

Welcome to Tillbridge Horse Stable and Guesthouse near Bolan, Maryland. As the sign just outside of town says, "Friends and Smiles for Miles Live Here." If you've visited before, welcome back!

I loved writing about the Tillbridge family and their friends, and I'm excited to see them again in the Small Town Secrets series. Rina Tillbridge's best friend, Philippa Gayle, was one of my favorite side characters, and I couldn't wait to share her story with you.

A slower pace, less traffic and a close-knit community are just a few of the reasons why Philippa enjoys living in Bolan and being the executive chef of Pasture Lane Restaurant at Tillbridge. Opinions and gossip are also a part of the package, but she's managed to keep her private life from becoming the next hot topic...until her ex-boyfriend celebrity chef Dominic Crawford comes to town.

Their history on a private island in the Caribbean years ago is revealed along with a few important secrets, including the fact that their feelings for each other are not as far in the past as they both thought.

A Chef's Kiss will take you down a road of secrets as well as friendship, a passion for food and enduring love. I hope you enjoy the journey.

Hearing from readers is something that adds a smile to my day. Instagram, Facebook and my newsletter are three of my favorite places. I hope to see you there. You can also find out more about me, the upcoming books in the Small Town Secrets series, as well as the connected books in the Tillbridge Stables series, at ninacrespo.com.

Wishing you happy reading!

Nina

A Chef's Kiss

—

NINA CRESPO

H HARLEQUIN

SPECIAL
EDITION

Recycling programs
for this product may
not exist in your area.

ISBN-13: 978-1-335-40832-7

A Chef's Kiss

Copyright © 2021 by Nina Crespo

All rights reserved. No part of this book may be used or reproduced in
any manner whatsoever without written permission except in the case of
brief quotations embodied in critical articles and reviews.

This is a work of fiction. Names, characters, places and incidents
are either the product of the author's imagination or are used fictitiously.
Any resemblance to actual persons, living or dead, businesses,
companies, events or locales is entirely coincidental.

This edition published by arrangement with Harlequin Books S.A.

For questions and comments about the quality of this book,
please contact us at CustomerService@Harlequin.com.

Harlequin Enterprises ULC
22 Adelaide St. West, 41st Floor
Toronto, Ontario M5H 4E3, Canada
www.Harlequin.com

Printed in U.S.A.

Nina Crespo lives in Florida, where she indulges in her favorite passions—the beach, a good glass of wine, date night with her own real-life hero and dancing. Her lifelong addiction to romance began in her teens while on a "borrowing spree" in her older sister's bedroom, where she discovered her first romance novel. Let Nina's sensual contemporary stories feed your own addiction for love, romance and happily-ever-after. Visit her at ninacrespo.com.

Books by Nina Crespo

Harlequin Special Edition

Tillbridge Stables

The Cowboy's Claim
Her Sweet Temptation
The Cowgirl's Surprise Match

Visit the Author Profile page
at Harlequin.com for more titles.

Chapter One

Six years ago...

Philippa Gayle buttoned her white kitchen jacket and brushed lint from her black pants. As she looked in the dresser mirror, she put on her chef's beret, tucking in her short dark hair, and adjusted the band until the monogrammed name of her hopefully would-be employer, Coral Cove Resort, showed clearly in front.

Last month in New York, she'd gone through two intense rounds of interviews for the position of sous chef at the exclusive property, beating out a dozen candidates to make it to the final stage—a month-long, paid interview audition.

Leaving her position as a cook at a hotel in Charlotte, North Carolina, and traveling to the private island just off the coast of Barbados was a huge gamble. But at age twenty-two, having a shot at her dream job made the sacrifice worth it.

Knocks echoed in the small bungalow.

Philippa walked from the bedroom into the adjoining living room.

The sun, just peeping over the ocean horizon and shining through the sliding glass door along the side wall, added a soft glow to the blue-and-cream decor.

Outside on the deck, Dominic Crawford leaned on the doorjamb. The breeze swaying the surrounding palms and yellow, flowering cassia trees plastered his blue button-down to his solid chest and ruffled the hem hanging over his tan shorts.

She opened the door, and the smile edging up his mouth and the intensity of his gaze stole words.

Madagascar cinnamon... His eyes were the same rich color of the spice known for its understated flavor, but there was nothing subtle about Dominic. He was six feet plus of dark-haired, naturally deep-tanned gorgeous.

Backing Philippa inside the bungalow, he shut the door behind him, grasped hold of her waist and kissed her. He faintly tasted of one of her favorite things—hazelnut-flavored coffee.

Sliding her hands up and around his neck, she fell into a kiss that sped up her heart rate.

If only she could forget about everything and just spend the day with him. But she was due in for the Friday breakfast and lunch shifts in the kitchen. And she couldn't be late.

Philippa eased out of the kiss. "Don't you have a boat to catch?"

"I do." Dominic briefly pressed his mouth back to hers. "But I think I left a shirt here. A long-sleeved white one. Did you find it?"

Sinking her teeth into her lower lip, she attempted to hide a smile. "I did. But it's wrinkled. I slept in it last night."

"You did, huh?" His grin, along with his short, dark, tapered hair, brought even more attention to his eyes and the taut angles of his face. "If you would have let me sleep here last night, you could have had me instead of the shirt."

Laughing, she half-heartedly held him back as he nuzzled her neck. Heat and the inviting scent of citrus and amber emanating from Dominic made him even harder to resist. "Sleep was the last thing on your mind. And what about Bailey?"

His older sister, Bailey, had arrived on the island yesterday morning. Dominic and Bailey were taking a water taxi from Coral Cove to Bridgetown, Barbados, that morning to meet their parents who were flying in from New York.

He huffed a chuckle. "She wouldn't have missed me. She was snoring in bed by nine last night. But

I'm missing you already. I wish you were coming with us."

"Even if I didn't have to work, it would have been wrong for me to intrude. It's your day off, and your family came to spend it with you."

"Intrude? Not even close. Once my parents get to the hotel suite, they'll spend the rest of the day working until it's time for dinner with one of their prospective clients."

His parents were financial advisors and ran their own firm. Twenty-seven-year-old Bailey, older than Dominic by two years, worked for them.

Dominic laid his forehead to Philippa's. "You could have sat by the pool with me and Bailey."

And that would have been as thrilling as being tossed into the deep end.

During dinner at Dominic's bungalow last night, a conversation she'd had with Bailey had felt more like a comparison analysis where, in Bailey's eyes, she'd come up short. .

Bailey had pointed out that Dominic had graduated from Johnson & Wales University's culinary arts program with honors. Philippa had completed a culinary arts program at a junior college in Atlanta.

Bailey had bragged about Dominic interning in kitchens with award-winning chefs during semester breaks, while Philippa had confessed to working part-time gigs from food trucks to pop-up restaurants to catering companies to help pay her tuition.

Later on, Bailey had been sitting on the back deck talking on the phone. She'd been unaware of Philippa walking outside to bring her a piece of ice-cream-topped chocolate cake.

Dominic has been with her since he's been on the island. It's no big deal. She's second-rate compared to him...

The self-doubt and negativity Bailey's remembered comment had stirred up then came back to Philippa now. Pushing them aside, she smiled up at Dominic. "It's just one day. We'll be together tomorrow."

"I know." He released an extended breath. "But we really need to talk."

Just as Philippa was going to ask what about, the reminder she'd set for work beeped on her phone.

Slipping from his grasp, she took it from her pocket and turned off the alert. "I better go. I want to get in early. You know how Chef LeBlanc is. I have to be ready for anything."

As she turned to retrieve his shirt from the bedroom, Dominic lightly grasped her wrist and tugged her back to him. "You *are* ready for anything. Remember that."

His sincerity made it easy to forget that they were rivals for the sous chef position.

From the moment they'd said hello to one another at the airport, waiting at the gate for the flight from Charlotte to Bridgetown, they'd been drawn to each other. In the days that followed, every glance, smile and conversation neither of them wanted to end had brought them closer.

Sleeping together had just naturally happened. But they were keeping things professional in public, always waiting until they were in their private bungalows to indulge their attraction.

She brought him his shirt, then nudged him out the sliding door. Before she shut it after him, he snuck in one last kiss. "I'll call you."

"You better." A short time later, smiling, she left by the front door and hurried down the palm-tree-lined path.

Ahead of her, employees who'd arrived by water taxi from Barbados walked into a three-story yellow building with white shutters known as the Hub.

Located near the center of the island, it housed support services, administrative offices, a suite of rooms for the general manager and a kitchen providing twenty-four-hour room service.

Philippa and Dominic had been placed in two of the resort's smaller bungalows so they could get a taste of guest life, but whoever got the job would have to live in Barbados.

In the Hub, Philippa found Executive Chef Liza LeBlanc on the delivery dock, checking over crates of produce.

The brown-skinned woman with family roots in New Orleans and Hawaii shifted her attention from the delivery man opening a crate of mangos to Philippa.

Philippa suppressed the urge to glance down and check if her uniform was in order. The other day, she'd missed tucking a strand of hair under her hat, and Chef LeBlanc had brought it to her attention.

Chef LeBlanc nodded to the delivery man that she would accept the mangos, but she waved away the crate of carambola. "It's nearly a full house. I hope you're prepared for a busy day."

"Yes, Chef. I'm ready."

"Good. I have paperwork to finish, so you'll be in charge this morning."

Nerves knotted and pulled inside of Philippa. Supervisory experience was one of the weakest areas on her résumé. This could be one of her last chances to impress Chef LeBlanc and the higher-ups with her leadership skills before they made their selection next week.

Philippa joined the staff in the heart of the well-equipped commercial kitchen.

Cooks prepared an array of orders from scrambled-egg combos to Bajan salt bread filled with succulent ham to thick, rich smoothies made with fresh fruit and vegetables.

Off to the side, butlers in crisp aqua-colored shirts and black knee-length shorts waited for the orders they would promptly deliver to their assigned guests.

During a lull in the service, she reviewed lunch tickets stacked in an in-box near the butler's station, searching for special requests. Today, they fell into the "none of this, less of that" variety.

Last week, they were more unconventional. One of the guests had requested a tuna melt made with blue cheese, drowned in hot sauce and served on crustless, extra hard, cinnamon-raisin toast every single day of their stay.

The sandwich had resembled a crime scene on a plate, but she'd added a carrot-rose garnish and personally handed the meal to a butler with a smile. The guests came first, and Coral Cove aimed to please.

A chime dinged on her phone tucked in the front pocket of her jacket.

The dark-haired butler standing next to Philippa sent her a slightly startled glance. "No personal distractions during a shift" was one of Chef LeBlanc's main rules and she'd just broken it.

Crap! Philippa fished out her phone.

On the screen was a selfie text from Dominic, smiling in the hotel pool with a green dinosaur floaty wrapped around his waist.

Barely suppressing a laugh, Philippa turned her phone to silent and put it back in her pocket. She missed him already. Once the interview audition was over, how would she handle not living just a bungalow away from him?

They hadn't talked about what would happen when the interview process was over. They'd stay in touch, wouldn't they? Was that what Dominic wanted to talk about?

At the end of her ten-hour shift, she removed her apron, tired and ready for a walk on the beach. Maybe she could catch Dominic before he went to dinner with his parents and find out what was on his mind.

"Philippa." Chef LeBlanc beckoned her.

Weariness followed Philippa to the corner office. Hopefully, a double shift wasn't in her future.

Chef LeBlanc sat behind the desk, her expression more stern than usual. "Have a seat."

Anxiety rippled through Philippa as she sat in the chair in front of the desk. Breakfast and lunch had gone smoothly. Was she in trouble for not remembering to turn off her phone?

"We received a complaint from bungalow five about their breakfast."

Chef LeBlanc slid an order ticket across the desk, and Philippa picked it up. "A tomato-and-spinach omelet and a high-protein, berry-and-kale smoothie. No added salt or sugar. I remember this one. I saw the omelet being prepared to order, and I made the smoothie myself. Was something missed?"

"The smoothie was supposed to be made with rice milk, but it was blended with soy."

An image of the red-lettered, soy milk container

in her hand as she made the smoothie flashed into Philippa's mind. Her mouth went dry. "I'm so sorry. I'll apologize to the guest right away."

"It's too late for that. The guest in bungalow five is the daughter of Coral Cove's newest investor. She complained to her father, and he called the general manager. I tried to convince them to give you another chance, but I was outvoted. I'm sorry, but this incident has taken you out of the running for the position."

Not sure she'd heard her right, Philippa sputtered, "So...my audition is over?"

Empathy came into the other woman's eyes. "Yes, I'm afraid it is."

Disbelief stunned Philippa into silence. She swallowed against the tightening in her throat. "Thank you for the opportunity. Working with you has been a great experience."

"You were impressive. Don't hesitate to include this interview audition on your résumé. I'm happy to give you a recommendation."

Chef LeBlanc taking an interest in her future displaced some of Philippa's sadness. "Thank you."

"I also have some advice, if you're willing to hear it."

"I appreciate any guidance you're willing to give me."

Chef LeBlanc sat back in the chair. "Managing a top-notch kitchen is a full-time commitment that comes with rewards and sacrifices. The reward is having your talent and creativity appreciated. The sacrifice is having to put most of your focus on the job. That doesn't leave room for much else…especially a personal life."

Was Chef LeBlanc just giving her general advice or did she know about her relationship with Dominic?

Philippa couldn't tell as she met Chef LeBlanc's steady gaze. "Thank you. I'll keep that in mind."

In her bungalow, fighting back tears, Philippa packed her bags on the bed. Messing up a simple ingredient change on an order. How had she made such a rookie mistake? But her relationship with Dominic had nothing to do with it. For the past three weeks, other than her hair being out of place and forgetting to turn off her phone, she hadn't made one major slipup until that morning.

Philippa's phone rang on the dresser, and she caught a glimpse of the caller ID on the screen. *Dominic.*

She wasn't ready to talk to him yet, not without getting all emotional. And now wasn't the time to break down and cry.

Per the agreements her and Dominic had signed at the start of the interview audition, as the unselected candidate, she had two hours to pack her things and leave. Human resources had already booked her a hotel room in Bridgetown near the airport. Her flight left in the morning.

Philippa let the call go to voice mail, but fifteen minutes later, Dominic phoned again.

She answered.

"Philippa…" Relief filled Dominic's tone. "Are you okay? I ran into one of the butlers in town. They told me what happened. I can't believe they're ending your interview audition over one mistake."

"But it was a big one. The guest was a VIP, related to an important investor. But I shouldn't have messed up in the first place." If only she'd reviewed the order one more time. Stuffing down sadness and disappointment, she shoved her work boots into a tight space in her carry-on. "I have to go. I need to finish packing. The next water taxi leaves in thirty minutes."

"I'll be waiting for you when it docks."

"Aren't you going to dinner with your parents?"

"You're more important. I'm staying with you tonight…and, hopefully, past the weekend. You could change your flight and we can hang out in Bridgetown or wherever you want."

"Don't you have to work?"

"I can't return to the kitchen until I officially accept the offer. I told Chef LeBlanc I needed a few days to think about it."

"But you're going to accept it, right?"

"Yes, but my answer can wait. We need to talk about us."

Spending a few days with him figuring out their relationship status did sound nice. And she could drown her sorrows in rum punch over not getting the job while helping him celebrate the offer from Chef LeBlanc. He was going to make a great sous chef. And someday, an even better executive chef.

Managing a top-notch kitchen is a full-time commitment... The sacrifice is having to put most of your focus on the job. That doesn't leave room for much else...especially a personal life...

Chef LeBlanc's words came back to Philippa. She'd assumed that guidance referred to her time at Coral Cove, but did it concern Dominic? He was about to accept an important supervisory position. According to Chef LeBlanc's advice, if he wanted to be successful, he couldn't afford the distraction of a relationship, especially a long-distance one. And if she wanted to achieve her dreams of running a top-notch kitchen one day...neither could she.

The truth plummeted inside of Philippa, and she sank down on the bed. "I can't stay."

"If you're worried about the cost of changing the ticket, I'll pay. You can return the favor when I'm traveling to see you."

"The cost of the ticket isn't the problem." Forming the words made Philippa's heart so heavy, she forced herself to breathe. "We had fun these past weeks. Trying to make it into something more is too complicated."

"Are you saying you want to end it?"

The image of Dominic smiling down at her that morning flooded into Philippa's mind. Had she known that would be the last time he'd hold her, she wouldn't have rushed the moment.

Philippa squeezed her eyes shut and willed the image away. "Yes."

Chapter Two

The present

Philippa bumped her hand against the white mug on her desk and coffee sloshed over the side. As she dabbed the spill with a napkin, the scent of the hazelnut-flavored brew intertwined with the smell of charred bread wafting into her office.

Burnt toast and spilled coffee—trouble is on the way...

She'd read that line in a thriller novel once. But for a restaurant, those two things weren't the kiss of death. Bad reviews were.

Philippa closed the labor report on the desktop in front of her and tossed the soggy napkin in the trash. She had a meeting in ten minutes, but she'd check in on the breakfast service first.

After slipping on the lime-green Birkenstock clogs just under her chair, she stood, put her phone into the side pocket of her black cargo pants and picked up her black leather padfolio.

A quick glance at her reflection in the tinted window overlooking the kitchen of Pasture Lane Restaurant, located at Tillbridge Horse Stable and Guesthouse, confirmed her green-and-black headband held her dark locs in place.

Beyond the glass, cooks in charcoal-gray uniforms and black ball caps prepared omelets and pancakes in the center cooking island. On the other side of the red-tiled space, more cooks chopped fruit in the corner prep area and took pans of baked muffins and croissants from the stainless steel, double ovens built into the wall.

A kitchen helper removed burnt bread from a conveyer toaster and quickly put fresh slices in the machine.

Philippa walked to the front of the kitchen to her sous chef at the expediter station, monitoring orders from the servers on a digital screen. "Everything okay, Jeremy?"

"Yes, Chef." The sandy-haired guy in his early twenties, who was just as passionate about weight training as he was cooking, took his attention from the screen. His usual confidence reflected in his blue eyes and his smile. "We're past the rush. Things are slowing down now."

"Good. I've got a meeting in the dining room. Find me if you need me."

"Will do." He went back to clicking through tabs on the screen.

Reassured Friday morning's breakfast service wasn't going up in flames, Philippa made the mental switch to her upcoming nine-thirty consult with the event organizer who had flown in from LA to Maryland last night. They were working on the plans for a fifty-person, private, advance-screening party for the futuristic Western, *Shadow Valley*, the movie that had been filmed at Tillbridge last year.

The Tillbridge family, who owned and managed the horse stable and guesthouse, were looking forward to the event and the soon-to-be-released movie. The film was not only good for business, but Tristan Tillbridge, one of the owners of the property, was married to Chloe Daniels, a lead actor in the film. Her visit to the stable early last year to research the part had led to the unlikely pair falling for each other.

But Cupid's arrow hadn't stopped there. His cousin and Philippa's best friend, Rina Tillbridge, had literally run into her stuntman soulmate, Scott Halsey, on the set one afternoon.

A few months later, Rina's sister, Zurie Tillbridge and deputy sheriff Mace Calderone, a family friend, had faked being engaged to hide Tristan and Chloe's secret wedding plans from the media. In the end, the two had discovered they weren't just pretending but were in love.

Tristan, Rina and Zurie had endured so much in the past, they deserved to find love. As the next generation of owners overseeing Tillbridge, they were finally getting a chance to rebuild their family's legacy and their own futures.

Philippa walked into the front of the restaurant and gave the casually dressed patrons occupying the tables a cursory glance. One person stood out in the pale, wood-floored space.

The event organizer, Rachel Everett, sat in a less-crowded area near the wall of glass. But unlike the other guests captivated by the sunny, springtime view of lush grass and trees beyond the wood deck, the slim strawberry blonde in a fashionable teal pantsuit remained absorbed in her phone.

Rachel still hadn't decided on the menu. And she'd turned down the offer of a tasting as part of their meeting. With the event just a month and a half away, they should have made more progress. Hopefully, this meeting would clear things up.

"Good morning, Ms. Everett." Philippa gave the event organizer a friendly smile.

A pleasant expression came over the young woman's face. "Chef Gayle—good morning. Thanks for meeting with me today. Again, I apologize for the short notice about my visit."

"Not a problem. I'm glad we're meeting in person to nail down the details." As Philippa sat down, she glanced at the untouched basket of breakfast pastries on the table. "Would you like to order breakfast?"

Rachel held up a half-full white ceramic cup. "No, thank you. I'm fine with just coffee."

After waiting a beat or two for Rachel to kick off the meeting, Philippa opened her padfolio and woke up her computer tablet. "Did you get a chance to look over the menu suggestions I sent?"

"I did," Rachel nodded. "They were…decent."

Decent? The word jabbed Philippa like the tip of a sharp knife. That's how leftover takeout was described, not her well-thought-out catering menu that had received high praise from customers.

Philippa moved past the lukewarm assessment. "If you have something else in mind, I'm happy to consider it. Or maybe we should squeeze in time for a menu tasting to make it easier to decide?"

"A menu tasting isn't necessary." Rachel's pert nose twitched. "The party just needs items with more…" The organizer's expression morphed from finicky to thrilled. "You're here!" Jumping to her feet, she hurried to someone behind Philippa.

"Sorry I'm late," he replied.

The man's deep, smooth voice rumbled through Philippa along with disbelief. *It couldn't be...* She looked over her shoulder, catching a glimpse of Dominic hugging Rachel.

Air squeezed out of Philippa's chest and her heart sped up.

The embrace ended, and Rachel laid her hand briefly on Dominic's forearm, just underneath the pushed-up sleeve of his burgundy shirt. "I thought you were arriving yesterday. What happened?"

Smiling, he tucked car keys into the front pocket of his jeans. "I had to take care of a last-minute VIP booking at the restaurant."

"Ooh." Rachel leaned in. "Who was it?"

Dominic's low chuckle raised goose bumps, destroying Philippa's hopes that maybe he was a hallucination. "You know I can't tell you those details."

"Can't?" Rachel gave a subtle eye roll. "More like won't."

Philippa faced forward as Dominic and Rachel exchanged small talk about his flight.

Was he working in the area? From Rachel's reaction, she'd been expecting him. What if Rachel introduced them? How should she respond? How would *he* respond?

Rachel's breezy laugh reached Philippa seconds before the planner and Dominic got to the table. "Anyway, you're just in time," Rachel said to Dominic. "Chef Gayle and I were discussing the menu for the party. She'll be working under you. I can't wait to hear your fabulous ideas."

Working under him? Hear *his* fabulous ideas? As the reason why Dominic was there struck Philippa, shock gave way to irritation. She looked up. "I thought I was in charge of the party?"

"There's been a small change. You do know who he is?" Rachel pointed to Dominic, who had a slightly stunned look on his face.

Did she know him? Star of the cooking show *Dinner with Dominic*, owner of the celebrated LA restaurant Frost & Flame, the author of two bestselling cookbooks and runner-up on the cooking reality show, *Best Chef Wins Los Angeles*, five years ago.

Like every other culinary arts professional who paid attention to the industry, Philippa had heard of Dominic's exploits. But she'd avoided watching his show or reading about him as much as humanly possible. Being with him had turned her life upside down in ways she'd never anticipated.

As she met Dominic's gaze, an echo of the passion, regret and the heartache she'd experienced after she'd left Coral Cove, because they'd been together, reverberated in her chest.

But that was in the past. She'd earned her way to where she was—at the top of *her* game—and no one was taking that away from her.

Philippa stood. "I know exactly who he is, and I don't care. I'm the executive chef here. I don't work under anyone."

Chapter Three

Dominic, still reeling over seeing Philippa after so many years, didn't know what to say. "Philippa... hold up..."

Ignoring him, she strode toward the double doors with two small windows located at the back of the dining area.

Dominic looked from Philippa to Rachel. "You didn't tell her I was involved with the party?"

Rachel held up her hand, holding back the censure. "It wasn't intentional. You coming on board for this event was a last-minute change. Holland just requested you two days ago."

Holland Ainsley, the director of *Shadow Valley,* was a big fan of his restaurant and was good friends with Bailey, who was his business manager. One call from Holland to Bailey, and the movie screening event at Tillbridge had been added to his schedule.

The papers he'd signed had mentioned a restaurant on the property but not the name of the chef. He'd assumed whoever was in charge was okay with the plan of him being there.

Invading another colleague's space was the last thing he'd ever anticipated happening. No, seeing Philippa was.

Frustration, on his and Philippa's behalf, raised tingles along the back of Dominic's neck, and he rubbed over the spot. "I don't care if it just happened. Someone should have given her a heads-up about my involvement. Or I should have been informed you hadn't talked to her about it."

"I couldn't mention it to her before you signed the contract, and it was only finalized last night. But would it have mattered? I take it you two have a history?"

Catching on that his silence meant he wasn't going to comment, Rachel sighed. "Fine. I'll handle it. When I meet with Zurie Tillbridge tomorrow, I'll make sure she knows that Chef Gayle is being difficult, and that you would prefer not to work with her."

"Don't." The firmness in his tone earned him a brow raise from Rachel. "I owe Philippa the professional courtesy of an explanation and an apology. Hopefully, she'll be willing to talk to me so we can come up with a solution that suits us both."

"If that's what you want. You're in charge of the party." Rachel slipped her tote from the back of the chair. "I'm on my way to New York to see another client. I'll be back here tomorrow morning for a meeting with Zurie. I need to know Chef Gayle's answer before then."

Rachel left, and as Dominic wove through the tables, headed for the kitchen, he received more than a few double takes from patrons.

People staring at him. It had started during *Best Chef Wins Los Angeles* and had become a constant now that he had his own show. Bailey always reminded him that it was a small price to pay for his success. Small or not, it still made him uncomfortable.

At the back of the dining room, a dark-haired server wearing a T-shirt printed with MY THERAPIST EATS HAY glanced at him as she cleared dirty dishes from a table. Recognition dawned in her widening eyes. She froze.

Hoping to break through the awkwardness, he flashed a fan-friendly smile. "Hi. Chef Gayle—is she in the kitchen?"

"Uh, yes." The server pointed behind her. "She's in there."

"Thanks."

He walked through the double doors, and as the staff noticed him, the noise lessened and activity slowed.

Near the center of the kitchen, Philippa stood at a metal table, chopping a chicken into pieces with a cleaver. "This isn't break time, people. Customers are waiting."

The staff reanimated, but many of them shot curious glances his way.

As he walked to Philippa, a recollection flashed through his mind of the two of them in the kitchen at Coral Cove. When they'd been in proximity, it had been difficult not to stare at her. Whenever she'd caught him, she'd smiled.

In the present, Philippa barely spared him a glance. "Guests aren't allowed in here. Let your server know what you need. They'll take care of it."

"I'd like to finish our meeting."

"Our meeting is over." She separated a leg and a thigh on a cutting board with one sharp stroke. "I'm no longer involved with the party." A slight southern lilt flowed through her words. That only showed up in her tone when she was stressed or irritated.

"I'd like to talk about the party. Privately. In your office."

He looked pointedly around the kitchen, and she followed his glance to her staff pretending they weren't listening to their conversation.

"Jeremy," she called out.

A muscular, sandy-haired guy came over to the table. "Yes, Chef?"

"Take over for me, please." After sharing instructions for what she wanted done with the chicken, she washed her hands at a small sink against the side wall.

At the entrance to Philippa's office, Dominic let her go in first. The faint alluring scent of sweet almond and shea butter trailed after her.

Emerging memories of smoothing sunscreen on her skin at the beach drew his gaze to her fitted chef's jacket, hugging her curves. Her favorite beachwear had been a burgundy bikini and a matching wrap she used to knot low on her hips.

A vision of her on the beach, laughing and untying the wrap, billowing and clinging to her sun-kissed toned legs, flashed in his mind.

He wiped the image from his thoughts seconds before she turned and faced him. "I'm listening."

"I'm sorry you weren't told that I was involved. That never should have happened. The director of *Shadow Valley,* Holland Ainsley, is a fan of my restaurant. She requested me."

Philippa's expression remained neutral.

Determined to get through to her, he added, "If I would have known you were here, I would have called to discuss partnering on the event."

"I appreciate the apology, but my answer is still

no. Two head chefs trying to manage an event never goes well. It only complicates things."

Too complicated was the reason Philippa had given for why they needed to break up six years ago. "We used to make a good team."

"Yes. We were a good team. But we're in different places now."

An insistent knock sounded at the door.

Frustrated over the interruption and Philippa's unwillingness to budge from her position, Dominic released a harsh exhale as he opened it.

In the doorway, Jeremy looked to Philippa. "Sorry for bothering you, but the dish-machine repair reps just walked in. You said you wanted to talk to them when they showed up."

"Thanks, Jeremy, I'm on my way."

As Jeremy returned to the kitchen, Philippa started to follow him.

As she passed by, Dominic gently caught her wrist, and a magnetic pull of awareness sucked a breath out of him.

From Philippa's wide-eyed look, he wasn't the only one who'd felt it.

He released her and let his hand fall to his side. "I'm staying here at the guesthouse until Sunday morning. Meet with me so we can work this out. Please."

Softness mixed with a hint of sadness came and went from her eyes so fast he almost missed it.

A resolute expression came over her face. "I'm sorry, Dominic, but I've already made up my mind. Good luck with the party."

Later on, Dominic walked into the single room with a king size bed, his conversation with Philippa in her office still on his mind.

As he set his black overnighter on top of the navy comforter and tossed his key card on the dresser, more distant memories settled in.

She'd insisted they were too different to work together. Six years ago, their differences had connected them.

At Coral Cove, he'd been more experienced as a leader than Philippa, but the variety of places she'd honed her skills and her passion for food had made her a formidable opponent. They'd quickly realized they could learn from each other and that they had a lot in common, sharing similar visions from taste profiles to the presentation of food.

Neither of them had questioned what would happen when one of them got the job and the other one didn't. From his perspective, all that had mattered was figuring out a way for them to stay together once Coral Cove's management made their decision.

He'd assumed Philippa was on the same page. Finding out she wasn't had been a gut punch.

You're right. It was just a temporary thing...

That's what he'd told Philippa. But for weeks after she left, he'd struggled to forget her.

One night, during that time, he'd even called her, but she didn't pick up. That's when he'd accepted their relationship was truly over.

As Dominic's thoughts came fully back to the present, the distant view outside the window of two horses grazing in a green pasture came into focus.

With increasing responsibilities and the odd relationship in his life, he'd moved on. But seeing Philippa today…

The question he'd wrestled with, after their breakup, needled his thoughts.

Had he really been the only one who'd felt something special had existed between them at Coral Cove?

As much as he hated to admit it, he still wanted to know.

Chapter Four

Philippa scrolled through the time sheets on the computer screen.

A management restructuring had happened a few months ago, and she was no longer in charge of the guesthouse *and* running Pasture Lane Restaurant. But having fewer employees didn't mean she wasn't busy. Running Pasture Lane involved ordering, maintaining inventory, reviewing the financials, monitoring the staff, and above all, making sure the guests were satisfied. She really didn't have time to worry about anything else…like Dominic being somewhere in the building.

A whisper of tingles moved over the place where

Dominic had touched her wrist, and Philippa rubbed the sensation away.

She'd thought about reaching out to Zurie to see if she knew about him taking over. But why interrupt Zurie's day off over this? The director of the film asked for Dominic, and as far as them collaborating, what she'd told him was true.

With the screening party for *Shadow Valley* just weeks away, they didn't have time to solve their idea-and-style differences. It made sense that she should step aside. That's what she'd explain to anyone who asked.

Not working with him had nothing to do with their past. She was over it. She never thought of him. Unless someone brought him up.

The first year after Coral Cove had been the hardest. For months, her mind had kept recycling thoughts of the two of them on the island, and just when she laid that all to rest, he'd been a contestant on *Best Chef Wins Los Angeles*.

At the restaurant in DC where she'd worked at the time as a lead cook, the staff wouldn't stop talking about the show or him. Apparently, he'd been a fan favorite, known for his confident-with-a-hint-of-cocky attitude and how good he looked in his chef's uniform. And her coworkers had also been caught up in his relationship with one of the show's contestants.

It had hurt to hear he was with someone, but putting Chef LeBlanc's advice in place, about remaining focused on her job, had tuned most of it out. And staying on task had helped advance her into a sous chef position at the restaurant.

The only other time Dominic had come up was a couple of years ago when Rina had purchased his first cookbook and kept raving to her about it. Telling Rina that she knew him and wasn't interested in his recipes had been the first time she'd acknowledged their acquaintance to anyone.

And then there was Chloe's bachelorette party last year. *Dinner with Dominic* had come up in the conversation, and everyone had raved about him... except her. Actually, Rina had been the one to bring him up then, too.

Philippa's phone chimed on her desk with a familiar ringtone. It was Rina. Why wasn't she surprised? "Hey, what's up?"

"Don't 'what's up' me. Why didn't you call and tell me Dominic Crawford was in the area? I had to hear it from one of my customers."

"It couldn't have been that important since you're just calling me now."

"I just got the chance. I've been running around so much I can barely keep up with myself." As a co-owner of Tillbridge and the owner of Brewed Haven Cafe in the nearby town of Bolan, Rina stayed busy.

"How's the new online ordering system working out? Things must be booming."

"The last few days have been a little hectic, but it's nothing we can't handle. Now, stop trying to change the subject and tell me about Dominic. Why was he at Pasture Lane?"

"You honestly don't know?"

"Why should I?"

"He's preparing the food for the screening party."

"Really? No one told me, but I missed Monday's meeting with Zurie and Tristan. Are you excited to work with him?"

"We're not working together. I've been replaced by him."

"Replaced? Since when? Did Zurie tell you this?"

"No. I found out from the event planner this morning, but I'm fine with not being involved. Two head chefs—"

"Hold on."

A muffled conversation between Rina and someone else came through the line.

Rina returned. "I have to go. They need me. Come by the house for dinner tonight. I want to hear the full story about this thing between you and Dominic."

"There is no thing between me and Dominic."

"Okay, then come over and tell me about the thing that's *not* happening between you and Dominic. I'm making spaghetti Bolognese."

"With fresh garlic bread?"

"Do you really have to ask? Seven thirty good?"

Philippa mentally ran through her schedule. She'd have to go there straight from Tillbridge. "That works."

"See you then." Rina ended the call.

Mumbling to herself, Philippa laid her phone on the desk. "I do not have a thing with Dominic."

Philippa shone a flashlight into the darkness illuminating the garden in Rina's backyard. "Have you found them yet?"

"No." As Rina walked farther down the row of plants, the yellow tie holding her braids and the matching Brewed Haven T-shirt she wore with a pair of jeans reflected in the light. "I know I spotted some red peppers out here this morning. Where are they?"

Relaxing on the couch with a glass of wine, wearing her T-shirt and a pair of borrowed sweatpants from Rina's closet—that's how Philippa had envisioned waiting for the delicious dinner Rina had promised. Not gardening in the dark.

Philippa swatted a bug flying near her face. "Do we really need red peppers?"

"Yes."

Leaves rustled on the bushes near the back fence.

Philippa swung the light that direction. "What was that?"

"Relax. It's probably just a couple of raccoons.

I saw them out here this morning...when I noticed the peppers."

Knowing Rina, being happily distracted by wildlife in her backyard was the reason she hadn't picked the darn peppers in the first place. "Hurry up or I'm giving the harmless, rabid raccoons the flashlight, and they can help you."

"As long as they hold the light steady. I won't mind. Found them." Rina sang out as she held up her claim.

"Good. Let's go." Philippa hiked across the yard toward the welcoming light shining from the white, two-story clapboard house.

Rina caught up with her. Humor was in her sepia eyes, and a wide smile covered her pretty brown face. "Why are you in a hurry to leave the garden? You always say fresh is best."

"Fresh vegetables are best, but normal people pick theirs in the daylight. Dinner better be worth braving the wild animals hiding out in your backyard."

Rina playfully nudged her arm. "You know it will be."

They went through the side door of the house into a small, lighted entryway.

Rina set the peppers on an empty built-in shelf, then pulled off her yellow boots with goofy-looking chickens printed on them.

After slipping off the pink-and-white, polka-dot

garden boots Rina had loaned her, Philippa followed her down the hall into the beige-and-white, country-chic kitchen.

The delicious smell of tomatoes, basil and garlic hung in the air.

After they'd washed their hands, Rina stirred the meat sauce simmering on the stove.

Philippa rinsed off the peppers in the sink. Surprisingly, Rina hadn't leaped on the topic of Dominic already. If Rina didn't mention it, she wouldn't. As far as she was concerned, the matter was closed. He was cooking for the party, and she was steering clear of him.

"How do you want these cut?" Philippa asked.

"Julienne strips. They're going into the salad that's in the refrigerator. The way the plants are growing, I'm going to have to give some of the tomatoes and peppers away. That plant-food recipe that the gardener at Sommersby shared with me is amazing. You really should have gone with us the other weekend. It was so relaxing."

Sommersby Farm Vineyard and Winery was located a few hours away from Tillbridge. Not only did they grow grapes and produce wine, but they also maintained a small orchard and a modest crop of seasonal vegetables that they served in the restaurant on the premises.

Philippa put the peppers on the white marble cutting board on the counter. "It was a couples' weekend for you and Scott and Zurie and Mace. Being there alone would have been awkward."

"I'm pretty sure you wouldn't have been alone. The gardener asked about you." Rina spread garlic-seasoned butter on the inside of a sliced baguette.

Philippa tried to picture him in her mind. "Is he the one I met at Brewed Haven?"

"You didn't just meet him. He asked you out. Too bad you didn't take him up on it. It might have made today a little less uncomfortable."

Philippa pulled a cutting knife from the butcher block. "What does the gardener have to do with today?"

"I just meant that if you would have been seeing someone, maybe your confrontation with Dominic wouldn't have been so dramatic."

"Dramatic? What are you talking about?"

"Someone told one of my servers that you told Dominic you wouldn't work with him if he was the last chef on Earth."

"What?" Philippa glanced at Rina. "Which someone is spreading that around?"

"It's not one particular person."

"Of course not." Philippa cut open a pepper.

It never was with gossip, and that was a huge part of the problem. Like the telephone game, the rumor started with one person, but by the time the story made the rounds, it was an insanely twisted version of the truth.

Rina popped the bread in the oven. "So I guess the part about you holding hands with him in your office isn't true either?"

"No, we…" Philippa paused in slicing the pepper. She and Dominic hadn't been holding hands. He'd been holding hers, sort of. But it could have looked like they were holding hands from outside her office. Especially since she hadn't pulled away. "What people are saying, it wasn't that way at all."

"But what went on today, does it have something to do with you and Dominic being in a past relationship?"

Philippa went back to cutting the peppers. She'd admitted only to Rina that she knew Dominic. Not that they'd been together. And still Rina's spidey-sense had homed in on something. "How long have you known?"

"For a while. Honestly, I guessed. Hearing Dominic's name always made you irritated or sad." Rina stood beside Philippa. "Whatever happened between the two of you, I could tell it went deep."

Gratefulness for Rina choosing not to pry despite what she suspected mixed with the need to finally tell the truth. "Six years ago, he and I were the last two candidates for a sous chef position at a private island resort. The interview audition was a month long, and we got close. I know. Don't say it. Getting involved with him under those circumstances wasn't smart."

"No judgment here. I'm sure getting together with him felt right at the time."

"It did. But it wasn't. I made a mistake with one of the guest's orders and was sent home a week early because of it."

"And you think the relationship was the cause?"

Philippa took the salad from the refrigerator and brought it to the counter. She hadn't thought so at first, but weeks after leaving the resort, it was clear. "Being with him impacted my future. I should have thought it through before getting involved with him."

"And now the party at Tillbridge has brought him back into your life. No wonder you don't want to be involved."

"No. Dominic is *not* back in my life. And I'm fine with him handling the party. It's better this way. Two head chefs trying to run things can be a pain. And I'm sure everyone will be a lot more excited about the event now that a well-known chef is preparing the food."

"I'll accept any reason you give, and so will Tristan and Zurie, but as far as everyone else…" Rina offered up a shrug. "You not being involved with the party might feed the belief that you hate him."

"I don't hate him." Philippa dropped the pepper strips into the bowl. "I just don't want to be…" *around him.*

Finishing the sentence in her head red-flagged the truth. Dominic had been her greatest weakness to date, and she wondered if he still was. What if the spark of awareness she'd felt when he'd touched her that morning mushroomed into something she couldn't ignore? What if she started remembering all of the things she'd worked so hard to forget?

Rina nudged Philippa's shoulder with hers. "Not wanting to work with your ex because it's too awkward is valid."

"But you're right. If I don't, it could fuel this silly rumor about me hating him and create more gossip. You know how I hate being involved in rumors."

Whispered conversations behind her back. Knowing smiles and innuendos. Even more-distorted versions of the truth being talked about around town.

Helplessness settled over Philippa. "What am I supposed to do?"

"I don't know what the right answer is, but I get it." Empathy showed in Rina's eyes. "My parents used to say tough choices are like a rainstorm. You can't stop it from coming, but you can decide how you're going to get through it."

Chapter Five

As Dominic talked on his phone to Bailey in California, he glanced out the window of the guest room at Tillbridge. Heavy gray thunderclouds shadowed the early morning sky. "I'm not doing the party."

"What?" Bailey's tone rose an octave. "You can't back out. We've already signed the contract."

"And I'm sure it has an out clause, just like every other contract you've negotiated for me."

"Of course it does." Bailey gave a derisive snort. "Did you really wake me up for this?"

Dressed in jeans, Dominic snagged a gray pullover from his overnight bag sitting on the bed. "I waited three hours to call you. I've been awake since 4:00 a.m., my time. I couldn't hold off any longer. Rachel needs to know I'm out of the event before her meeting at Tillbridge early today."

"We're not telling Rachel anything. You can't make a decision like this on a whim."

"I don't do things on a whim, and you know it. If the situation had been handled properly with Philippa in the first place, there wouldn't be a problem."

"Ahh, the truth emerges. I'd wondered how long it would take before she became an issue."

Dominic paused before putting on his shirt. Bailey knew about Philippa being there? "The only truth that's emerged is that you held back information from me. Why didn't you mention Philippa was the chef here before I signed?"

"What happened between you two was in the past and it was personal. Signing this contract is about what's taking place now—a business opportunity—and how much money is on the table."

Money. Was that all Bailey thought about? Sometimes he wondered if giving a damn about anything other than a lucrative contract had been completely removed from her DNA. As financial advisors, not even their parents were that single-minded about money. Was Bailey adopted?

"I don't care about the money." He sat on the bed to pull on his black high-tops. "I care about me being used in a way that treats Philippa unfairly. It wasn't right."

"Right or not, this situation isn't just about you anymore. Once you agreed to become involved, Holland and her people upped the ante for the event. It's gone from fifty to a hundred and fifty guests donating a lot of money to see the film plus an exclusive, deleted scene, added back in, just for this audience. She's giving the proceeds from the event to her scholarship fund for women in film. And we've made a bigger commitment, too. The production and creative teams have already moved forward with the plan to film farm-to-fork episodes of *Dinner with Dominic* in Maryland."

One of the things that had excited him about the screening party was the access to local farms near Tillbridge. He'd envisioned developing a menu for the event featuring fresh food and preservative-free ingredients sourced from the area. Tying the menu to a few special episodes of his show had been a perfect fit. Or at least it had been until the situation with Philippa.

Last night, he'd thought about taking another shot at changing her mind, but he kept coming back to her two-head-chefs-managing-an-event excuse. It was flimsy, and it pointed to one explanation that went beyond contracts. Philippa didn't want to work with him. Period.

He'd encountered jealousy and animosity from rivals, and he hadn't cared, but Philippa's refusal to collaborate… That struck in a way he couldn't just shake off.

"Look." Hints of exasperation hung in Bailey's tone. "Could the way you were brought on as the chef for this party been handled differently? Absolutely. Can I get you out of this contract and smooth things over with Holland by making a huge donation to her scholarship? Probably. But there are influential people in her circle who won't be so forgiving. When you first started out in LA, Holland endorsed you. Not returning the favor by doing this event will come across as—"

"Ungrateful."

"Or selfish. You're the chef everyone wants to hang out with. No one wants to be around the chef who has his own hit show but won't help film students in need."

"I am willing to help but not by doing the party. I'm sure you and the new publicity firm you just hired can put another spin on it." Or at least they should, considering how much he was paying them.

"We could try to swing it around with a few rumors about Philippa being the difficult ex-girlfriend. You not wanting to bring that type of negativity to a positive event would definitely gain you sympathy points."

"Whoa, hold up. You will not spread rumors about Philippa. Put the blame on me."

"And tarnish your reputation right before we're

about to enter into contract negotiations for the show *and* drop the announcement about you opening a restaurant in Atlanta? Don't think so. I know the whole running-into-your-ex was a curveball, but you have to set that aside and think about our investors, along with everyone who supports the show."

People depending on him seemed to be the reasoning for every decision he made. Dominic closed his eyes a moment, trying to envision a time when that wasn't the case. He'd been carrying the responsibility so long, he couldn't.

"Well, then." Bailey yawned and gave a relaxed sigh. "I'm going to get a couple more hours of sleep. Think about the angles. I'll hold off on calling Rachel. Bye."

Bailey ended the call. From the lightness in her tone, she assumed she'd won the argument. Maybe she had.

His brand. His reputation. And what was believed about him, true or not, impacted the people around him and not just the ones he employed. Now it had affected Philippa, too. She'd been moved aside by Rachel so he could take over the movie event.

Fighting a tiredness that tempted him to lie back on the mattress, Dominic rose from the bed and grabbed his phone and wallet from the nightstand. Making decisions half asleep and hungry always made him cranky. He needed food and coffee.

Dominic went to the door. As he walked out, he pulled up short to avoid running into someone.

Surprise flitted across Philippa's face as she remained poised to knock. She lowered her hand. "You're here. Good."

Dressed for work in her chef's uniform, Philippa blew past him, and her alluring scent trailed after her.

She crossed to the other side of the room near the window and faced him. "I want to talk about us working together on the *Shadow Valley* screening party."

Confusion over why she was there, along with jetlag, made him slow on the uptake. "You said you weren't interested."

"I know, but I might be with a few stipulations."

They were negotiating. That was an improvement.

He shut the door. "What did you have in mind?"

Philippa paced near the window. "First, we oversee the production of assigned items with separate teams."

"That's reasonable. Splitting up the menu is more efficient." And from a who's-in-charge perspective, it would eliminate the issue of her working under him.

"Second. My staff is excited about the possibility of meeting you and maybe working with you during the party. Their eagerness is understandable, but it's also a distraction."

A distraction for them or her? He set his things on the dresser, leaned back against it and crossed his arms over his chest. "What's your solution for that?"

"Well, of course, I don't have a problem with members of my staff working the party. That was part of my plan, along with bringing over workers from the Brewed Haven Cafe. But I think the excitement of you being around would die down if you did something special for the staff, like a cooking demo. You could answer their questions, and sign autographs."

So she wanted him to play the part of celebrity chef. It was an expectation he'd come to accept. But from the tension emanating from Philippa, she was the one playing at something. Was she not at ease with her suggestions, or was she not at ease with him?

Philippa paused, awaiting his response.

He shrugged. "I don't have a problem with that either."

"I also think trading sous chefs and lead cooks during the planning of and during the event itself would be an advantage. Our people are familiar with how we work. They can meet on our behalf, if we're busy, and help keep us in sync during the event. And having the experience of working with you is something my staff will be able to add to their résumé."

"Trading staff sounds like a good idea, too." Dominic uncrossed his arms and pushed away from the dresser. He ambled over to Philippa. "And I'm sure my sous chefs will find it just as beneficial to learn from you. Maybe they could team up with your people in Pasture Lane's kitchen a few nights while they're here. Experiencing how another operation works is always valuable."

"I don't have an issue with that."

"Good. It sounds like we've made progress." Dominic took a step closer.

As she stared back at him, softness filled her eyes, and he glimpsed the Philippa he used to know. The woman who'd been passionate about food and her convictions about life. A passion he'd felt whenever he'd kissed her and held her in his arms.

Philippa's gaze dropped from his. She intertwined her fingers in front of her so tightly, her skin grew taut over her hands.

Was she concerned about her proposition? He was on board with all of it. As if reacting to muscle memory, his own fingers slightly twitched with the urge to cup her cheek and reassure her they were in a good place in their new working relationship.

Dominic tucked his hands in his front pockets. "I'll let Bailey know what we've discussed. She'll ask Rachel to draw up a new contract outlining the terms. Unless you'd prefer to initiate things?"

"No, that's fine. But I do have one more thing to ask."

"Name it."

Philippa lifted her head. Resoluteness filled her expression. "This alliance is strictly professional. Our past doesn't factor into it. There's no need to talk about Coral Cove."

"That's fine with me. As a rule, I don't talk about my private life with other people."

"I don't just mean we won't discuss Coral Cove with other people. We won't talk about it with each other. Ever."

What she'd just spelled out about them working together, along with not talking about Coral Cove lined up in his thoughts, revealing a pattern. The terms she'd set minimized their contact, limited their communication or kept them apart.

Take the win... Bailey's practicality laced through the voice in his mind.

He'd gotten what he'd wanted—a solution that kept his image intact, took care of everyone who depended on him and was also fair to Philippa.

But it didn't feel like a win. Avoiding their past or pretending it never existed felt like a betrayal of what they'd meant to each other six years ago.

But it was only a betrayal to him, wasn't it?

Philippa hadn't felt the same way about their relationship. And he needed to accept that.

Taking physical steps away from Philippa and mental ones from their past, Dominic walked to the dresser for his phone. "If that's what you want. That's fine with me. I'll text Bailey now. You'll have a new contract by tomorrow."

Chapter Six

A week later, animated conversation traveled over the hustle and bustle of the kitchen into Philippa's office. She paused in working at her desk and looked out the window.

Cleaning up after Saturday brunch, the staff was more jovial than usual, their excitement palpable over what was taking place in a little over an hour. Dominic's cooking demo.

Jeremy and the dark-haired, lead line cook, Quinn, laughed as they conferred with Teale and Eve, the culinary producer and production designer for *Dinner with Dominic*.

The two women on Dominic's staff were setting up the demo and helping with the development of the menu for the private screening party. They had arrived earlier that week with the advance team to scout out locations to film segments of the show.

Teale, an upbeat twentysomething with short brown hair and a generous smile, had been the one to tell her they were filming episodes of *Dinner with Dominic* in the area.

The last time Philippa had spoken to Dominic was that past Saturday in his guest room at Tillbridge, when she'd outlined her terms for them working together.

He'd left the next day without saying goodbye, but as promised, the new contract had arrived on her desk. Once she'd signed it, things moved at lightning speed.

That Monday, the sous chefs Dominic had assigned to work with her for the movie screening event had called to introduce themselves.

An assistant also emailed Dominic's notes for the party. His farm-to-fork theme had reminded her of the conversations they'd had at Coral Cove about their dream restaurants. They'd envisioned visiting farms and local producers to find what they needed to create dishes full of natural flavor. Did he remember that?

But she'd never know if he did recall those moments, since they weren't talking about the past. Or maybe they weren't interacting directly at all. So far, their meetings, including the one tomorrow morning, were group meetings with him and his team.

He was keeping things strictly professional... just like she'd asked.

A sudden restlessness came over Philippa. The laughter reverberating through her office added to her aggravation. She needed to clear her head and stretch her legs.

She left her office and veered left instead of right. Walking past the dish room, she went out the side door at the rear of the kitchen. In the light-tiled, white-walled hallway, staff in blue coveralls navigated cleaning carts onto the service elevator.

Farther down, she shared a brief smile with a red-haired groundskeeper on a ladder, swapping out a flickering florescent light bulb.

She exited the hallway, entering a wide corridor behind the lobby of the guesthouse.

A couple examined tourist brochures in a gold-tiered literature stand.

Philippa amped up her smile to customer friendly and exchanged hellos with them.

She passed a shorter adjoining hallway where the business center, a meeting space and the fitness room were located. Up ahead on the left corner was the closed, glass double-door entrance to Pasture Lane Restaurant.

A green paper, printed with the notice that the restaurant was closed for the rest of the afternoon and would reopen for dinner at five, hung on the inside of the door. She should look in on the setup before Dominic arrived. But honestly, she probably didn't have to check. Earlier that day, everything had been ahead of schedule.

Jeremy, Quinn and Teale, all in their early twenties, had hit it off as soon as they'd met, and Eve, a Black woman in her fifties who radiated health and self-confidence, fit right in with them. They clicked as a team.

Jeremy and Teale were at the point of finishing each other's sentences...just like her and Dominic had at Coral Cove.

Not ready to go into the restaurant yet, Philippa kept going and made an immediate right.

Tile transitioned to polished dark-wood flooring. Gold-framed paintings of horses running and grazing in rolling fields and near mountains hung on white walls.

Up ahead, close to a small seating area off to the side, Dominic smiled as he took pictures with a group of people.

He's already here... Philippa's heart stuttered with a spark of happiness. She reversed her steps around the corner.

Curiosity made her peek back at Dominic and the crowd.

The charcoal chef's jacket and pants he wore

looked tailor-made for him. Paired with his dark boots, he made a sexy fashion statement.

The warmth of excitement blossomed inside of her. It wasn't that she was glad to see him. She was just happy that he was able to make it.

Philippa glanced down at her own lime-green chef's jacket and black pants. They didn't look new like Dominic's clothing. And her pants had a dusting of flour on them. She'd jumped in to make more Belgian waffle batter during brunch. Doing so had freed up a kitchen worker to start cleaning a bit earlier so they could be ready to attend the demo.

"Boo!" The unexpected greeting came with a tap on her shoulder.

Philippa barely stifled a shriek. "Rina, what the…?"

Dressed in her Brewed Haven T-shirt and jeans, Rina had undoubtedly come directly from the cafe. She laughed. "Who are we peeping at?"

"I wasn't peeping at anyone."

Rina squeezed past her to check for herself. "Oh, I see. You weren't peeping. You were drooling."

"I was not." Heat fused into Philippa's cheeks. "I was on my way to the front desk, and when I saw him with guests, I didn't want to interrupt."

"All of them aren't guests. The woman pushing ahead of everyone, she works as a groomer at the doggie day care spa in Bolan. Wait, all the groomers from the spa are here, and the owner is, too. And that guy works at the wine shop."

"They must have camped out in the lobby and waited for him." Philippa looked over Rina's shoulder. "I'm surprised they got in. Zurie sent out a memo about extra security being around while Dominic and his team are here. They're supposed to control access to the guesthouse."

"Actually, I'm surprised the lobby isn't packed. I've been fielding questions about him all week. Good thing he's not the type who shies away from attention."

Dominic waited patiently as a middle-aged woman who worked at the dog spa pulled two of his cookbooks from her bag.

His smile was genuine and his demeanor easygoing as he signed them, then took more pictures and chatted with his fans.

Rina nudged her. "There's Zurie."

Crisp and efficient-looking in a white blouse, navy slacks and matching pumps, Zurie exuded an all-business mindset and a natural, inner radiance.

In her late thirties, she and Rina had the same delicate features. As she greeted a few of the locals, her dark hair swung near her shoulders.

Spotting Philippa and Rina, she walked over to them.

"I was just coming to find you," Zurie said to Philippa. "Did you hear the news?"

"No." Philippa glanced briefly to Rina for a clue, but she just offered up a shrug.

"Dominic and his people wanted more exposure for this afternoon. They leaked his arrival and handed out special passes for the demo."

"This was supposed to be for my staff. Something casual with minimum setup."

"I know." Zurie sighed. "By the time I heard about it, things were already in motion, so we just have to deal with the situation. It's only twenty to twenty-five people, but you have nothing to worry about. I was assured that Dominic's team would handle rearranging the set up."

Philippa held back a response. Whether or not Dominic's team were handling the adjustments wasn't the problem. The changes were made without anyone consulting her. And what about her staff? They were looking forward to having direct access to him. Had she known this was how Dominic and his team operated, she would have spelled out her definition of collaboration in the contract.

Philippa turned toward Pasture Lane. "I still better check on things."

Zurie laid a hand on Philippa's arm, stalling her departure. "They also scheduled a meet and greet with Mayor Ashford and some of the town's officials in the conference room after the demo."

Rina snorted a laugh. "By town officials, you

mean his entire family. After last week's town hall meeting, you might need referees."

Referees? That didn't sound good. "Why? What happened?" Philippa asked.

"What didn't happen?" Zurie shook her head. "It all started when the mayor's brother-in-law, who's on the school board, accused his ex, who just took a position in public works, of having the crosswalks painted off-white instead of bright white, and according to him they're crooked."

"He also said she did it just to annoy him," Rina added. "Forget about going to the movies for entertainment. Just bring a bag of popcorn to the next town hall meeting and pull up a seat."

"You got that right." Zurie gave Rina a knowing look. "Lately, the level of drama has been unbelievable."

Actually, it was highly believable. With many of the mayor's immediate and extended family holding key positions in Bolan, it wasn't the first time a meeting had resembled a family squabble. But they also loved to schmooze with important people. As a celebrity, Dominic was catnip for them.

"I'll make sure the meeting room is ready." Philippa put the task on her mental checklist.

"And there's one more thing," Zurie said. "Now that this is a bigger deal, someone needs to introduce Dominic before he starts the demo. Dominic's publicist and I think you should do it."

And the hits just keep on coming... "Why me?" Philippa asked. "I don't know him that well. Sure, we used to know each other, but that was a long time ago."

Zurie shot her a puzzled look. "You don't have to know him to read his bio. And you were the one who invited him to do this."

She'd asked him as part of their agreement. And she'd clearly spelled out the expectation. This demo was supposed to help decrease her staff's starry-eyed excitement over him, not increase his exposure.

Philippa glanced over her shoulder and ran into Dominic's gaze. He smiled at her, and she struggled to take her eyes off him.

Looking away, she broke from the trance. He was in celebrity-chef mode. Promoting himself. Doing his job. That smile had nothing to do with her.

Dominic's legs tensed as he suppressed the urge to go after Philippa. He adjusted his stance and smiled as he autographed one of his cookbooks for a fan.

Philippa had looked bothered, and he could probably guess why—the change of opening the cooking demo to the public.

This was Bailey and the new publicist's doing. He hadn't found out about the so-called "minor adjustment" until three hours ago, after his plane had landed at the airport in Baltimore.

He rarely got a moment that was less about him promoting his brand and more of a conversation about food, cooking techniques and career advice, like he and Philippa had outlined in their emails that past week. He'd been looking forward to the low-key demo. And seeing Philippa.

How had things gotten twisted around so damn fast with the demo?

Once again when he talked to her, he would have to apologize over something that shouldn't have happened. He would have rather started a conversation about her recommendations for the party. They were perfect.

Her suggestion to feature an upscale menu with a casual feel to reflect the mood of the event fit perfectly with the farm-to-fork theme he had in mind.

He'd longed to call Philippa and tell her that, and work through a few details about the recipes with her, but he and Philippa weren't that close. They didn't brainstorm ideas anymore. She wanted to move through the next few weeks as if how they'd interacted before had never happened. That they'd never anticipated each other's thoughts and next steps like they were their own.

Right then, she probably thought he was on board with making the demo more about him and less about her staff. He needed her to know that it wasn't that way at all. Even though he wasn't happy about them ignoring their past, it was important to him that she was comfortable with their present working relationship. He had to talk to her before the demo started.

In between signing autographs, Dominic glanced around the area. Amber, the publicity assistant the firm sent down to handle the event—where was she?

Somehow Bailey had managed to clone herself as the young woman who was probably just a minute or two out of college, all the way down to her chin-length wavy hair. Amber had even given him Bailey's patented death stare before reminding him he couldn't walk away from the crowd on his own when he felt done with signing autographs. He had to wait for her to pull him out so he didn't come off as the bad guy.

Minutes later, he spotted the petite young Black woman wearing a plum-colored business suit. She was busy talking on her phone.

He gave a subtle head tilt toward Pasture Lane, letting her know he was ready to go.

She lifted her finger and nodded, indicating he needed to wait a minute.

Dominic smothered impatience and turned his attention to a woman with short dark hair and silver poodle earrings, nudging people aside to squeeze in beside him.

"Can I get a photo?" she asked.

"Of course." He leaned in closer to the woman, and as she took the picture with her phone, he flashed a camera-ready smile.

A few more photos and autographs later, Amber appeared at his side. She raised her voice above the hubbub reverberating around them. "Thank you for coming. Dominic has to prep for the demo now. Those of you with tickets should remain here in the lobby until the doors to the restaurant open."

A groan of disappointment rose from the crowd.

Dominic waved goodbye. "Thank you, and thanks for watching the show."

Uniformed security for Tillbridge deftly stepped between him and the crowd as he followed the young woman into Pasture Lane.

In the dining area, a long, blue-cloth-covered table with portable burners and a smokeless table grill had been set up toward the back along with metal cabinets for heated and chilled foods.

Bethany, the blonde servers' supervisor he'd met the last time he was there, worked with her people. They arranged the light wood tables, most of which were clustered near the demo area.

Teale, dressed in a black, logo embroidered *Dinner with Dominic* pullover and red-and-black chef's pants with a flame design, approached with a huge smile. "Good. You're here."

"And you can relax," Eve, also in the same-style

crew uniform but with blue-and-black pants with a frost design, chimed in. "We're good to go with the changes. We were also able to find the last-minute ingredients we needed in Pasture Lane's kitchen to make the peanut-crusted bourbon chicken and the no-bake cheesecake shooters."

"But it wasn't easy." Teale mocked wiping her brow. "We owe Jeremy big-time for helping us."

"Bourbon chicken and cheesecake shooters?" Dominic frowned. "Those recipes are from my cookbook. I'm featuring items from Frost & Flame's current menu."

"We had to make another minor adjustment." Amber interjected. "I know you were planning to talk more about technique in a restaurant setting, but now that we have the general public in the room, we need the focus to be more relatable, like what's in your cookbooks."

Dominic faced Amber. "Any other adjustments I need to know about?"

"Just a couple of small ones. VIPs will be at the front table to your right as you face the audience— the mayor and his wife, the head of the local chamber of commerce, the fire chief. And on the left, there will be a table with a couple of food reporters from DC and a local journalist and her photographer. The rest of the tables near you will be guests who are staying at Tillbridge and locals from the area. The restaurant staff will be in back. Oh, and as a surprise, we have cookbooks for the VIPs and special invites."

"Hold on," he said. "This demo was originally scheduled for the staff. Why are they sitting in the back?"

"The special invites have tickets. They're expecting the royal treatment."

Dominic barely held back his irritation. "The staff who just worked their tails off to serve brunch and then clean up so I could do this demo for them also deserve the royal treatment."

Amber offered an apologetic shrug. "I know it doesn't seem fair, but if we don't give the VIPs and special invites prime access, there could be a backlash. They could talk to the press."

Teale quirked a brow. "And what about the employees of this restaurant? You think they won't?"

Dominic stalled their conversation with a raised hand. "There's only one thing I care about. The promise I made to Chef Gayle, and we will deliver on it."

Amber opened her mouth as if to object, then her shoulders fell with an exhale. "Okay. I'll make it open seating, except the VIPs and journalists have to sit up front. But the cookbooks—we couldn't get a larger number here in time. I had to make an agreement with the bookstore in Bolan to borrow from their stock and replace them before your book signing there next week. Maybe we can take care of the staff later."

He shook his head. "Later isn't good enough. I don't want them treated like they're second-class to everyone else."

"I may have a solution for the cookbook situation," Eve spoke to Amber. "Why don't we talk about it and let these two work on the specifics for the demo?"

As Eve guided Amber away, Dominic released a measured breath.

Teale studied him. "You okay?"

"I've been better. I know this situation has taken up a lot of your time. When you and Eve volunteered to handle this demo for me, I didn't anticipate things going sideways."

"Really?" Teale laughed. "We absolutely did. Last-minute details always pop up when publicity is involved."

Her positive attitude restored a bit of his optimism. "Thanks for rolling with the changes."

Eve and Teale's ability to handle challenges was what made them good at their jobs.

They'd been with him for over three years, almost from the start of *Dinner with Dominic,* and had been instrumental in helping him establish the basic premise of the show. Him and interesting guests, such as creatives, adventurers and innovators, cooking a meal together at the guest's house and talking about life and experiences. Their conversations explored a range of topics. Ways to make a difference in the world. Comic book icons. The dos and don'ts of dating. What makes life an adventure? Is it okay to be insecure about today and optimistic about tomorrow? Best movie lines ever.

The episode always ended with him, the guest and a few friends kicking back and enjoying the food they'd prepared.

Teale's creative vision was instrumental in coming up with food-and-drink themes to match the topics of the show. She also assisted with development of Frost & Flame's seasonal menus.

Eve, the organization whiz, made sure they had the right cooking tools, equipment and ingredients as well as dishes for showcasing the food.

Minutes later, Teale had him up to speed on the setup for preparing the chicken dish and cheesecake shooters along with the brown-butter lime shrimp that had originally been on the demo menu.

Jeremy walked out of the kitchen with a bowl of parsley. "Hey, Chef." He spoke to Dominic, but his gaze quickly settled on Teale. "You mentioned you might need more of this. I found some in the prep walk-in. We've got more coming in tomorrow."

"Great. Thanks." Teale beamed up at Jeremy.

"You're welcome. I'm happy to help." Jeremy grinned back as he followed her to one of the food cabinets to put the parsley away.

Dominic suppressed a wry chuckle.

The sous chef wouldn't be the first to become distracted by Teale. Hopefully, the guy wouldn't have issues concentrating over the next few weeks. Otherwise, Philippa might not be happy about that. Where was she?

Dominic cleared his throat as he walked over and interrupted them. "Have either of you seen Chef Gayle?"

"I think she's in her office," Jeremy replied. "But the blinds are closed. That usually means she doesn't want to be disturbed."

But this was his only chance for a quick check-in with Philippa before the demo started. With all the unexpected shifts in the presentation, letting her know that despite the addition of an outside audience, her people would have most of his attention was worth bothering her about.

Amber strode over to him. "I have a compromise. I got my hands on some numbered tickets. We'll hold a drawing for a few of the cookbooks. After the demo, the VIPs will get some one-on-one time with you in the meeting room down the hall. You'll autograph the cookbooks I've set aside for them, take some pictures and then meet with the journalists."

"That sounds reasonable." Dominic glanced back at the double doors leading to the kitchen. There went his chance to talk to Philippa.

"Good. The cookbooks for the giveaway are in an admin office. You need to autograph them with a generic signature."

Dominic followed Amber. The give-and-take of satisfying the public and the press, that was his part of the compromise for the demo. But so was making sure Philippa was satisfied. Hopefully, he could accomplish both.

Chapter Seven

Philippa fastened the last black button on her crisp new lime-green kitchen jacket, then pulled down the hem with a snap. So much for a simple staff presentation. Not only was she expected to introduce Dominic, per Zurie's request, she now had to stay for the entire demonstration and possibly hang out afterward with him and the VIPs.

The change of events also interfered with the plan of her taking care of prep for that night's main dinner entrées. She'd wanted to prevent her cooks from having to scramble to get things ready after Dominic's demo.

She didn't have time for this type of Hollywood-style hype. He had a large team to do the work on his show and at his restaurant. She was a chef in charge of a busy restaurant with a modest-sized staff. Something Dominic and his people obviously hadn't taken into consideration when they upscaled the event.

Philippa snatched the empty packaging for the jacket from her desk. Underneath it was the bio for Dominic that his publicist had dropped off not too long ago.

Chef extraordinaire. Bestselling author. Star of an acclaimed cooking show. A pampered chef focused on his public persona. Was that who she was dealing with for the next few weeks?

She tossed the packaging in the trash and picked up the bio. After opening the blinds covering the window, she stepped out of her office.

A few of the staff walked by.

"I don't care what he makes," one of the blonde servers said to a thin, lanky kitchen helper. "I just want to hear his voice as he describes it. He could make mud pies sound irresistible."

Philippa kept her face neutral as she followed behind them, but inside, she gave an inner eye roll.

"I'm just glad he's not a disappointment in person, like some celebrities," the kitchen helper responded. "The way he stood up for us about where we could sit in the dining room proves he actually cares about people who work in the kitchen."

Stood up for them? Was there not enough seats?

When she'd checked on things with Dominic's team and her staff, they'd said everything was good.

Philippa flagged down Quinn, who was walking past.

As usual, whenever Philippa talked to her, a slightly startled look came into the young woman's wide gray eyes. "Yes, Chef."

"I heard something about there being a problem with seating for the demo," Philippa said as she and Quinn walked toward the dining room. "Is everything okay?"

"Oh, yes, it's fine now." Quinn nodded quickly as she smoothed a strand of curly ebony hair behind her ear. "There was just some mix-up with the publicity person. She said all the Pasture Lane employees would have to sit in the back and let everyone else sit up front. But Dominic set her straight. And Eve said we're getting some cool *Dinner with Dominic* swag next week. Kitchen towels, water bottles, that kind of stuff."

"Oh? That's nice." When she and Dominic had talked about the demo, he hadn't mentioned giving her people swag.

"It is. It's so exciting that he's here. I can't wait to see what he's cooking for us today."

As Quinn rushed into the dining room, Philippa hung back and peered through the window near the top of the right-hand door.

Her staff sat intermingled with the rest of the attendees.

"How does it look out there?"

The resonant tone of Dominic's voice coming from behind her ignited a frisson of awareness that moved along Philippa's spine and tingled across her nape.

"It's a full house." She calmed an unsteady breath and faced him.

Up close, he looked even better than he had in the lobby. But hints of fatigue were in his eyes. Last week, he'd flown in after working at his restaurant the night before. Had he done the same this weekend? She hadn't taken his present work schedule into consideration when she'd asked him to do the demo.

"Thank you..."

"I'm sorry..."

They both spoke at the same time.

Dominic gestured for her to speak first.

"I appreciate you adding this to your full schedule. And for making sure my staff have front-row seats. If they weren't already fans of chef extraordinaire, Dominic Crawford, they are now."

He grimaced. "Chef extraordinaire?"

She'd meant to tease him, but from his slight wince, her attempt had fallen flat. "That didn't come out right. I didn't mean it in a bad way." Philippa held up the paper in her hand. "I was just referring to the intro Amber gave me."

"I should have guessed." He smiled, but as he glanced at the paper a shadow of discomfort moved across his face. "You don't have to say all that. Owner of Frost & Flame is fine."

"And have Amber come after me? No, thank you."

Dominic huffed a low chuckle. "Yeah, she's insistent." He took a step forward and the subtle notes of his cologne wafted into the space between them. "About the changes with the demo. I—"

The door opened behind Philippa, pitching her forward, and her hand with the paper landed on his solid chest.

Dominic took hold of her arms. "You okay?"

As she looked into his eyes, familiarity washed over her. The automatic desire to lean into him almost overwhelmed her.

Amber peeked past the door. "Chef Gayle, good. You're right where you're supposed to be."

Averting her gaze from his, Philippa moved out of Dominic's grasp. "Is it time?" The high pitch of her voice made her clear her throat.

"Almost. We're still waiting on the mayor," Amber replied. "I'll tap on the door when he's arrived. Oh, wait. He just walked in..."

"Good. He's here." Heart tripping in her chest, Philippa slipped past Amber and hurried out the door.

The mayor settled into a chair at a table on the right.

As more people in the audience started to notice her, noise decreased in the room.

Philippa plastered on a smile. "Good afternoon, everyone. Welcome to today's demo." She willed her fingers to open, unclenching Dominic's bio in her hand. "Chef extraordinaire, Dominic Crawford…"

He definitely felt extraordinary a minute ago… Giving herself a mental shake, she put aside the memory of how hard his chest had felt and his heat seeping into her palm.

When she finished reading the bio, the audience applauded, and she moved closer to the side wall.

Dominic came out the double doors of the kitchen. Smiling, he walked behind the table set up for the demonstration. "Alright. Are we ready?"

"Yes," some members of the audience responded, while others cheered and clapped louder.

Rina came up beside Philippa and deftly nudged her toward an empty table.

"What are you doing?"

"Saving you from yourself and a ton of rumors. You look like you're about to make a run for it."

"No, I don't."

"Tell that to your face."

As they sat down, Philippa flashed a cheery smile. "Is this better?"

"In a stalker-clown kind of way."

"I can't win with you. But how I look doesn't

matter. No one in this room is here to see me. They're here for him."

Exuding magnetic charm and swagger, Dominic picked up a sauté pan and set it on one of the burners. "Alright. Let's do this. I'm going to make you two of my favorite dishes. And then I'm going to top it off with something sweet. First up, peanut-crusted bourbon chicken. The key to making good food is quality ingredients and seasonings that enhance their natural flavor."

Dominic chopped, cut and mixed—a perfectly choreographed dance that he explained step-by-step.

Philippa couldn't stop herself from being drawn in as she watched him. Her kitchen helper had been right. The smooth, confident tone of his voice had an almost seductive quality that made his description of the food sound incredible.

Dominic took the browned chicken from the skillet and placed it in a shallow baking pan. "This needs to finish cooking in the oven." He handed the pan to Teale. "We'll sample this in about twenty minutes. Next up is a dish that's popular at Frost & Flame—brown-butter lime shrimp with Carolina Gold rice grits…"

That dish sounded familiar. Years ago, Dominic had been perfecting recipes that he'd jotted down in a notebook. She used to tease him about how many times he'd tweaked the brown-butter-and-citrus combination for multiple seafood recipes.

Soon, a citrusy, buttery scent filled the air. It was as if she could taste the tang of the lime juice Dominic mixed in with the nutty, rich taste of the browned butter.

A short time later, samples of both entrées were passed to the audience.

Philippa immediately took a bite of the shrimp dish. The reality of the flavors she'd imagined with the shrimp and the creamy risotto-like texture of the rice grits lifted her to a state of food bliss. And the herbs—he'd figured out the right combination.

Happiness for him made her smile.

Rina nudged her. "I know, right? You can't help but smile, eating this food."

A smile and the hmm... What did he used to say? *If you get those two things from someone after they've taken the first bite, you know you've gotten it right?*

As Dominic whipped up the chocolate cheesecake shooters, he opened the floor to Q&A.

"What inspired the theme for your restaurant?" someone in the audience asked.

"Years ago, I worked at a resort on the beach. The sunrises looked like fire hovering over the crystal-blue waves. It reminded me of fire and ice..."

Just like with the shrimp, another memory emerged in Philippa's mind of her and Dominic sitting on the beach together at sunrise, snuggled in a blanket. She could see his vision—the foam on the waves of the blue ocean had looked like ice under the fiery-orange rays of the sun.

While the island had awakened, they'd talked about everything, including wanting their own restaurants. New York, DC, Miami, Atlanta. Those were the places they'd envisioned themselves carving out their futures. Not Hollywood or a small town outside Baltimore. They'd made plans but the unexpected had unplanned their dreams.

"Chef Crawford. I'm Anna Ashford, senior reporter for the *Bolan Town Talk*."

The mayor's sister-in-law, a blonde in her late thirties, wore what she considered her uniform, a dark blazer with pushed-up sleeves over a T-shirt. Today, she'd paired it with jeans, and no doubt she also had on boots that looked new but were artfully worn as if she'd traveled miles in them instead of just up and down the streets of Bolan.

"I'm one of the few who has access to the private movie screening." Anna's attitude oozed with privilege. "I'd love to know if any of the items you prepared today will be served at the party?"

"Senior reporter?" Philippa whispered. "Isn't she the only reporter?"

"I guess she gave herself a promotion," Rina whispered as she got up. "And as much as I would love to stay and hear her riveting questions, I have to get back to Brewed Haven. See you later."

"Bye." Philippa gave Rina a small wave. No one said she had to stay for this part of the demo. Maybe she could escape, too.

Anna continued to dominate the Q&A. "How does it feel to be reunited with our very own Chef Gayle? That private island resort you just mentioned. Weren't the two of you there—together?"

Philippa froze midrise from the chair. Surprise and unease halted the air in her chest. What had Anna dug up about them? Whatever it was, he had to shut it down. Completely. As the audience's attention shifted between her and Dominic, Philippa sought out his gaze.

His attention remained on Anna as he flashed an affable smile. "Yes, Chef Gayle and I were both at Coral Cove. As far as the screening party—it's always a privilege to collaborate with a colleague and a talented chef."

Both at Coral Cove? Why had he mentioned the name of the resort? All he'd done was pour gasoline on the gossip fire Anna was trying to start.

"Well," Amber interrupted, "unfortunately, our time has come to an end. Let's show some appreciation for Chef Dominic Crawford."

The audience applauded.

Philippa stood, planning to leave the restaurant

by the front, avoiding Anna or anyone else with questions.

A few steps from the table, Amber zoomed in front of Philippa. A tight smile cut across her face. "Chef Gayle, would you mind coming with me please? I really need to talk to you about the setup for the meet and greet."

"I was just going there now." Philippa pointed to the front exit.

"We should go through the kitchen." Amber laid a hand on her back and nudged her that direction.

Their speed walk was a blur as the crowd got out of the way.

Annoying Anna moved toward them, took one look at Amber's face and backed up.

Inside the kitchen, Amber led the way to the back past the dish room and out the side door.

Dominic stood in the corridor.

His gaze met Philippa's. Before she could question what was going on, Amber motioned that they should walk farther down. They stopped near a corner at the end of the hall, and Amber pinned them both to the wall with a stare. She reminded Philippa of someone, but who?

"What is Coral Cove and what happened there?" Amber asked.

Dominic gestured to Philippa that she should answer.

Caught off guard, she responded with the first

thing that came to mind, "Well…it's a resort. We worked there…"

"It *was* a resort," Dominic clarified. "Now it's an aquatic research station."

Philippa tried to imagine the elegant resort no longer existing. "Really? When did that happen?"

"Two years ago," he replied. "The owners—"

Waving her hand, Amber cut him off. "I don't need to know the history of the place. What went on with the two of you while you were there? Were you just friends or more than friends?"

"We were more than friends," Dominic replied.

"Just friends," Philippa asserted at the same time. Did he forget that they weren't talking about their relationship?

Amber shook her head. "No. You need to decide what you want that local reporter and every media outlet covering celebrity entertainment to know. Until you get your stories straight, if anyone asks you about Coral Cove, your answer is you were both there. You're old acquaintances, and it's a privilege to be able to collaborate with each other as colleagues. Period. Don't elaborate." She looked to Dominic. "During the meet and greet, I'll handle the journalist from the *Bolan Town Talk*."

"Got it. Can you give me and Philippa a minute?"

"Sure. But make it quick." Amber walked down the corridor, the sharp clicks of her heels echoing on the tiles."

"What was that?" Philippa asked.

"That's a publicist's assistant who's ticked off that we were caught off guard by a journalist."

"She's not the only one." Philippa faced him. "Why did you give Anna the name of the resort?"

"I didn't. She mentioned private island resort. Nine times out of ten, she already knew the name, and if she didn't, as a journalist, she was going to find out."

"Anna isn't a journalist. She's a nosy woman who eats gossip for breakfast, lunch, dinner and a snack, and all you've done is given her an appetite for more about us." As Philippa paced, she lifted her hands then let them drop back to her sides. "The reason I agreed for us to work together was to *not* bring attention to us or our past relationship. And now you've ruined everything."

Dominic's brows shot up. "I ruined everything? You mean your master plan of us working together *not* bringing attention to us? Exactly how was that supposed to work?"

"It was a master plan." His skeptical expression fueled an outburst. "Don't give me that look. You don't know what it's like to live in a small community. Nothing ever happens here, and when it does, like a celebrity chef coming to town, everyone is all over it. That may be great for you, but as someone who knows you, that sucks for me. Especially since there's some silly rumor floating around about me hating you and us holding hands in my office yesterday."

"You think I don't understand?" A laugh shot out of him, but irritation flickered in his eyes. "Los Angeles is the ultimate big little town when it comes to rumors. It's the reason why I have a publicity firm on my payroll. One that could have handled this if you and I would have talked about Coral Cove in the first place."

"Oh, so this is my fault."

"It's not about fault. It's about fact."

"Fact? What fact?"

Dominic strode over to Philippa.

He leaned in near her cheek, and she immediately detected the exact notes of citrus in his cologne. *Mandarin*. "The fact that we can't forget about our past."

Opening her mouth to object, she drew in a deep breath, and her breasts nearly grazed his chest. Philippa's traitorous heart leaped with excitement.

Dominic moved back to look at her face, and the intense longing in his brought a rush of warmth to her cheeks.

Dropping her gaze, she stalled on his full, kissable mouth. Her own tingled in remembrance of the firm pressure of his lips, teasing and coaxing hers to open to him. The slow drift and glide of his tongue, drawing her into a deepening kiss. As desire pooled inside of her, Philippa dragged her gaze back up to his.

Want and frustration were in Dominic's eyes as he quirked a brow with an I-told-you-so expression.

A buzzing vibration came from near his hip.

Shaking his head as if in answer to an internal question, he stepped back and took his phone from his pocket. "It's Amber."

Philippa took several steps back as she fiddled with her collar, letting in a bit of cool air. "The VIP meet and greet. You should go."

Dominic moved as if to take a step forward, but as if sensing she needed distance, he paused. "We can't pretend it didn't happen. Coral Cove…us."

He was right.

Philippa tamped down the last of her weakening resistance. "When do you want to talk?"

Chapter Eight

Dominic sat on the end of the rectangular table in the meeting room at the guesthouse.

Teale, Eve and Matt, one of the show's location scouts, sat with him.

The meet and greet with the VIPs after the demo had ended an hour and a half ago. After the gathering, they'd commandeered the room to discuss plans for the farm-to-fork episodes of *Dinner with Dominic*.

As Matt went over the details of the locations where they were planning to film segments of the show, Dominic adjusted his position in the navy-padded chair and glanced at his phone.

5:15 p.m.

Philippa was supposed to meet him at seven, but she'd sent a text earlier letting him know that she would be late. Something had come up at Pasture Lane. Would she make it, or was this her way of trying to get out of talking with him?

She'd been so adamant about them not speaking about Coral Cove when she'd agreed to them working together. After the local reporter's questions, hopefully she realized they couldn't avoid the topic any longer. And then there was what had happened between them in the hallway after the demo.

He'd only planned to challenge her belief that nothing existed between them. To give her a small nudge by proving a point. But then he'd almost kissed her. It had taken everything inside of him not to slide his arms around Philippa and bring her closer. From the look on her face, she'd been willing to go past that line, but he wasn't. Not as long as she was in denial about their situation.

Matt shifted his dark-rimmed glasses from the top of his lightly tanned, shaved head to his thin nose. He flipped through notes on his tablet. "The second bee farm is further away from here, but it's worth the effort. Easier access, more room to set up our trailers. And based on what we discussed at our last meeting, it ticks more of the boxes as far as what we want to feature with the farm-to-fork theme—hive science, an organic garden, honey tasting. Oh, and the owner claims she's psychic."

Teale gave him a WTH look. "And one *other* benefit to consider is they have the best chili-infused honey I've ever tasted. I'm definitely seeing it woven into the screening menu."

"Chili-infused honey at a psychic-owned bee farm. Can't pass that up." Dominic chuckled. "Just make sure the permit situation looks good. Since we're on a tight schedule, we don't want to invest time and energy into something that's a long shot instead of closer to a sure thing. I'm sure Jill feels the same way."

Jill Allen, the director of the show along with Brianne, the assistant director, had both expressed concerns about the timeframe for filming the episodes.

"Locations is on it," Matt replied, referring to the team led by his boss, the locations manager. "But getting permits and fees on all the places on our list looks really promising."

"Oh?" Teale raised a brow. "Did the bee psychic tell you that?"

"No." Matt grinned. "I just don't think we'll have any hiccups."

Teale, Eve and Dominic joined Matt in knocking on the table to ward off bad luck.

Next, Eve briefed them on the status of the studio kitchen.

At first, the production team had tossed around the idea of taping the informational segments at the bee farm and other locations in Maryland and then filming the actual cooking segments in LA. But doing it all in Maryland was a better fit since they were planning to use local ingredients and would have to ship them to LA for the cooking segments.

Trying to find a suitable place had been difficult. But Eve and Teale, who'd been sharing one of the two-room cottages at Tillbridge, had come up with the idea of using a cottage to film the show.

As it turned out, the Tillbridges were in the process of remodeling the cottage Tristan Tillbridge used to live in. The empty space was the perfect blank canvas to create a temporary studio. It would also become their base of operations, and he'd sleep there instead of the guesthouse.

A half hour later, the meeting ended.

In high spirits, Teale, Eve and Matt gathered their things. They had plans to hang out at the Montecito Steakhouse, the local spot just outside town.

As Dominic rose from the chair, he glanced at his phone. No other texts from Philippa had popped up. They were still on to meet up in a little over an hour.

What was the best approach with her? Ease into the conversation? Listen to her first? Go all-in with the facts and share some solutions? Philippa was so closed off from him. It was hard to know which way to go.

Eve handed him the key card to the cottage. "Security started guarding the cottage this morning.

They also have a set of keys. As far as inside the place, I've already blocked off what will go where in the kitchen. The refrigerators came in today. And the guesthouse staff brought in some furniture."

"Good. Maybe I'll move there now instead of tomorrow night."

"You can, but apologies in advance. You won't have much privacy tomorrow, especially in the morning. They're installing the lights, and in the afternoon, the cabinets and the kitchen island. The appliances are being delivered, too. Work crews will be in and out for most of the day."

"Not a problem." Dominic slipped the key card into his front pocket. "First thing in the morning might be a good time for me to look around." Last weekend, he'd been too busy with work to take in the view. So far, he'd only seen the pastures and horses from a car or the guestroom.

Eve paused before going out the door. "And there's a surprise for you in the fridge at the cottage. The cocktail mixers you're supposed to taste test—they arrived this morning. I stored them there instead of one of Pasture Lane's walk-ins."

"Thanks."

He'd forgotten he was supposed to do that today. The company that made the handcrafted products wanted Frost & Flame to feature them at the bar and consider possibly serving their mixers exclusively.

Tasting them was his last work task of the day.

But he could use a break. If he hurried, he could pack his bags upstairs and reach the cottage before sundown. He might even have time to take a short walk before meeting with Philippa. Would she mind meeting him there instead of upstairs?

He sent Philippa a text about the cottage.

Walking down the corridor, he went by Pasture Lane Restaurant.

A small group of people engaged in animated conversation stood outside the glass doors preparing to walk inside.

Dominic kept his head down and veered right toward the modern lobby with country-living accents.

A man and a woman in navy button-downs with the Tillbridge logo—a white horse and *T* with a lasso—stood behind the curved reception desk assisting guests.

More people sat in a seating area furnished with two blue couches surrounding a stained natural-wood coffee table.

No one noticed him. *So far, so good...*

For now, he could get away with not having constant security. Once they started taping segments on location, guards would have to monitor the area to prevent interruptions.

As he got on the elevator alone, his phone rang. *Bailey...*

It had been a long day. He just wanted to relax until it was time to see Philippa.

Dominic sent Bailey a text.

Busy.

The doors shut as Bailey responded.

Okay. Call you tomorrow. First thing.

The doors reopened as another text came in.
Philippa's response to his question about the cottage.

I'll meet you there.

Chapter Nine

Sitting in the driver's seat of her red four-door, Philippa stared at her text message to Dominic on her phone.

An expensive package on her doorstep that she had to pick up. A pounding migraine that wouldn't go away. A moody, hungry goldfish that she had to feed. All of them were plausible excuses for her to send him another text backing out of the meeting. She'd have to buy the goldfish.

But a convoluted version of her and Dominic's history together appearing in the *Bolan Town Talk* was even more intimidating. They needed to get their stories straight, just like Amber had said.

A short time later, she arrived at the back of the cottage.

Uniformed guards from Tillbridge unclipped the metal cord barring entry to the driveway.

She'd stayed there a few months ago after a heavy rainstorm caused severe flooding and she couldn't get home safely. The guesthouse had been full, and the only space available had been the cottage.

At first, being stuck there on her first two days off in ages, and not being able to catch up on laundry, had been frustrating.

But then Zurie had sent over food and personal items and forbidden Philippa to go anywhere near Pasture Lane. She'd watched Netflix, ate when she was hungry and slept like the dead. When she'd left the cottage, she'd felt recharged.

Philippa parked behind a black SUV, then got out, leaving her purse in the car.

As she walked toward the back door, it opened. Dominic stepped out on the small porch wearing a brown T-shirt, jeans and casual boots.

Suddenly, she felt underdressed in her work cargo pants, fitted gray T-shirt and the gray-and-green tennis shoes she'd exchanged for her clogs.

He tucked his hands into his front pockets. "You made it."

"Sorry I'm late."

"That's okay. I know how it is, trying to leave the

restaurant on a Saturday night. I'm glad you were able to make it."

He let her go in first.

Philippa walked down the back hallway and stopped at the entrance to the kitchen.

Track lighting illuminated the semigutted, beige-tiled space. A refrigerator was the only appliance. The white marble counters were bare except for a single-cup coffee maker tucked off to the side. The cabinets had missing doors, and there was a space where a kitchen island used to be. The adjoining living room with polished wood floors was completely empty.

"You're staying here? But they're still renovating."

"Yes." Dominic glanced around. "But the bedrooms are done, and it will look more like a set kitchen tomorrow after they install the island and bring in the appliances."

"Set kitchen? You're taping your show here, too?"

He nodded. "The team looked at other places, but this one suits our requirements. We can mold it temporarily into what we need since it's empty. And it's a win for the Tillbridges, too, since we're footing the bill. Once we're done, it won't take much to convert this to a standard kitchen. Basically, they're getting an upgrade out of the deal. Do you want to sit?"

She was about to ask *where* when she spotted the

tall white bistro table with chairs in the adjoining dining area. Bottles and a package of small plastic cups sat on top of it with a small notebook. "Sure."

As they got closer to the table, she could read some of the labels on the bottles. "Pomegranate habanero, tomato watermelon, mango pineapple. What are these?"

"They're cocktail mixers. The company that makes them wants us to feature them at the bar in the restaurant. I didn't know how long you would be, so I was just about to taste test them. I could use some help."

"Sure. But I have to skip the alcohol. I'm tired and I'm driving."

Dominic chuckled, a rich deep sound that made her feel warm all over. "Not a problem. Non-alcoholic is the way to go for me, too, if I want to get up in the morning."

"Do you have ice?"

"Sure do. I'll get it. Can you set up the cups?"

She took a seat in one of the tall chairs that were next to each other and removed cups from the package.

He returned with napkins and an ice bin with two bottled waters resting inside of it. "Which mixer do you want to try first?"

"I think I need a warm-up before I try anything with habanero in it. How about the mango one?"

"Let's do it." He set the things he carried on the

table, then sat in the chair. The wide position of his legs and his broad shoulders shrank the space around them to the size of skin-tingling intimacy.

They sampled the mango-pineapple mixer first, taking sips of water in between as they moved through the rest.

Clearly in business mode, his expression was deeply contemplative as he asked Philippa her opinion about the taste and texture of the products and jotted down her answers. The notebook was well used.

Dominic had a notebook at Coral Cove, too. He'd used it to scribble down ideas and new recipes. He hadn't been so serious while doing it. But he hadn't been running his own enterprise back then.

Dominic sipped water from a bottle. "Which one is your top choice?"

"The mango-pineapple one. You?"

"The tomato-watermelon mixer surprised me. The sweetness of the watermelon and the savoriness of the heirloom tomatoes really comes through. And that hint of basil right underneath. That's not easy to achieve with a bottled product."

As Philippa looked at him, she caught a glimpse of the younger Dominic, itching to set the world on fire. And he had.

He quirked a brow. "What?"

"Your excitement about what you're doing. It's

grown even more. Choosing to pursue a career in Los Angeles was the right move for you."

"Los Angeles has been good to me, but a career there wasn't the plan."

"But you auditioned for a reality television show."

He stacked their used cups. "Actually, I didn't."

"So how did it happen?"

"I was visiting a friend in New York. Someone videoed me showing off in the kitchen making a stir fry—cutting vegetables, flipping the food in the pan. They posted it online, and it went viral. A scout for the *Best Chef* franchise saw it, tracked me down at Coral Cove and offered me a spot on the show. It was an opportunity to experience something different, so I went. But it definitely wasn't what I expected."

"What do you mean?"

"Well, for instance, you watched an hour-long show…"

Actually, she'd never watched a single episode of any of his shows, past or present, but there was no need to tell him that.

"But for the contestants, that was actually a twelve- to fifteen-hour day, not only planning recipes and cooking but also filming scenes or waiting around on set as the crew taped everything from multiple angles. And *Best Chef Wins* isn't about cooks preparing food, or the competition. It's about entertainment. The producers create the narrative for the contestants and their relationships with each other, true or not." A hint of bitterness entered his tone. "The more conflict, the better."

She had no idea the drama on cooking shows was so contrived. "That must have been hard."

"It was eye-opening." Dominic gave a barely there smile. "During the show, I was too caught up in trying to keep pace with the day-to-day to notice. It was afterward when I saw their true motives. I was portrayed as the cocky but likable one of the group. And who did everyone supposedly confide their fears to, only to privately worry on camera how I might use the information to win the competition?"

"You."

"Exactly. Of course I didn't, but when someone lost to me, they always blamed it on me knowing their weaknesses."

And what about his relationship with one of the contestants. Was that real or fake? No. That was none of her business and had nothing to do with what they needed to discuss.

Philippa tightened the twist tie on the package of cups. "I misjudged you this afternoon. You do know what it's like to have people fabricate things about you."

Chuckling wryly, he sat back and rested a booted

foot on the bottom rung of the chair. "Yeah, I do have a little experience in that department."

"So how do you think we should handle our situation?"

"Amber has already gotten the ball rolling. She's finding out what could entice this journalist from the *Bolan Town Talk* away from our story, at least for a little while longer."

"A lingering case of food poisoning would be better than dealing with Anna. She almost ruined Chloe Daniels's engagement to Tristan Tillbridge."

"We can handle her. We just have to control the narrative."

"And how do we do that?"

"If the subject of us comes up in an interview or even a casual conversation, we just have to tell *our* story, as close to the truth as we're willing to get."

Our story... The way Dominic said it sparked recollections of the passion they'd shared. And the wonderfulness of letting go and losing herself in it.

Dominic shifted on his chair. His leg brushed hers, and she shivered as she pulled herself out of the memory.

"You're cold?" He stood. "You should have told me. I'll turn down the AC."

As he walked to the control panel on the other side of the room, Philippa continuously hit the delete button in her thoughts. No. She shouldn't notice the muscles rippling underneath his T-shirt.

Or the way his jeans fit with the right amount of snugness, showcasing his long legs and all of his wonderful assets.

Needing to do something with her hands and her wandering gaze, Philippa focused on tidying the table. "Do you want these in the refrigerator?"

She picked up two of the mixers and swiveled around to get up. Hands full, she bumped into him.

"Oh!" Philippa bobbled the bottles. The top to the mango-pineapple mixer popped off sloshing orange-colored liquid on her chest.

"Whoa." As she started to lose her grip, Dominic stepped forward and made a grab for the mixers. "I've got it."

Bottles trapped in both of their grasps between them, the back of his hand grazed the tip of her breast. Tingles radiated and her breath hitched. *Headlights.* She had them. Philippa clutched the bottles tighter.

He did, too. "You can let go."

Let go of the bottles? Nope. She would just hold on to them. *And do what?* Keep them in front of her breasts all night? Nothing unusual about that, right?

Giving in to cold, hard reality, she released the bottles.

Dominic turned and put them on the counter.

Hands dripping with mango-pineapple mixer, she plucked the front of her T-shirt from her body, a futile attempt to hide her full-on high beams. "Sorry, I made a mess."

"I'll clean it up. Are you o—" Dominic glanced over at her. His gaze dropped to her chest, and for a few long seconds, he didn't blink. "You need a shirt."

He strode toward the beige-carpeted hallway.

She hesitated. It wasn't like she could refuse. Or leave. They still hadn't worked out a game plan for explaining their past connection.

Past? Ignoring the naysaying voice in her head that had shades of Rina's cackling laughter, she followed Dominic.

Instead of entering the main bedroom at the end, he went into the bedroom on the left.

She waited on the opposite side of the hall, near the bathroom.

Moments later, he came out with a sky-blue T-shirt.

"Here you go." Offering a quick smile, he handed it to her.

"Thanks." Philippa ducked into the bathroom and shut the door.

Taking off the shirt, but leaving on her black sports bra, she cleaned up the best she could with a white hand towel.

As she slipped on Dominic's T-shirt that fell low on her thighs, the fresh smell of laundry soap enveloped her instead of his wonderful cologne. A small pang of disappointment hit.

Stop. What are you thinking? Of course, he wouldn't give you a shirt he'd recently worn and hadn't washed yet.

As she scrubbed the stain out of her own, the soft fabric of his shirt brushed over her skin. She conjured up the image of that very shirt taut against him. Suddenly it felt like she was standing over a hot stove instead of a bathroom sink.

Setting aside her T-shirt, she splashed cold water on her face. After wringing out her shirt, she hung it on an empty towel rack to dry.

Philippa walked out into the hallway and toward the kitchen.

With his back to her, Dominic wiped down the counter. He'd changed his shirt to a burgundy one.

He glanced over his shoulder and just stared at her.

Even from a distance, she could see the tightness angling his jawline. And the longing in his eyes.

He'd mentioned that to solve their problem with Anna, they had to get as close to the truth as they were willing to get. But what would defining their feelings for each other cause or possibly cost them? They had to figure it out.

She walked into the kitchen, and he turned away from her, bowing his head. As he gripped the edge of the counter, the muscles in his arms grew taut.

Philippa came up behind him and reached out.

As her hand grew closer to his back, she could feel tension radiating from him.

She flattened her palm below his shoulder. "Dominic."

He lifted his head. "Philippa, I can't—"

"I know."

"No, you don't." Frustration edged his tone. "You have no idea what it's like for me to see you after six years and find out I still care about you. And you don't understand what it's like for me to be near you and have to accept that you don't want to feel anything for me. And you don't know what it's like to have to pretend that doesn't matter."

She'd hurt him. But that hadn't been her intention. Unsure of what to say, Philippa wrapped her arms around him from behind. His unsteady breath vibrated into her cheek. "It does matter."

Dominic turned to face her and she let him go. Longing burned even brighter in his eyes. As if testing the waters, he slowly lowered his hands to her waist.

When she didn't move away, he slid his hands to her back. "What are you saying?"

"I was pretending, too. I was afraid of what would happen if I let you know how I really feel. I don't want to be afraid anymore."

Tired of trying to maintain a distance between them, she let the barriers drop. As she raised on her toes, Dominic wrapped his arms around her, and the press of his lips to hers was like a homecoming, heady, sweet and long overdue. She glided her hands up his chest to his nape, and he brought her closer, melding her to his muscled torso. The evidence of his need pressing urgently against her belly made Philippa moan into a deepening kiss that took her back to what they'd shared on the island. Real, uninhibited passion.

Dominic picked her straight up, and as he carried her through the living room into the hall, she wrapped her legs around his waist.

A feverish kiss interrupted the journey and when he set her down just short of the bedroom, she backed him up against the wall.

"Off," she murmured against his lips, tugging up the hem of his shirt.

Dominic pulled it over his head and came back in for another kiss.

Philippa caressed his hard chest and skimmed over the ridges of his abs, absorbing the heat rising from his skin. Him without the shirt was only a taste and not nearly enough. She unfastened his jeans and reached for the tab of his zipper.

Dominic took hold of her hands. "Not yet." The huskiness of his voice vibrated into her.

His open-mouthed kisses down the side of her neck made her shiver in anticipation.

Lifting her up, he carried her into the bedroom.

In one quick, smooth movement, he backed her down on the bed.

She sank into the mattress, welcoming his weight along with the sweep of his lips and his bare palm gliding over her belly as he nudged up her shirt and bra. Molding his hand to the curve of her breast, he sucked the peak past his lips.

"Dominic…" She sighed his name, losing herself in the lush heat of his mouth.

He unfastened her cargo pants, and the downward slide of his palm made her heart speed up. As Dominic moved past the barrier keeping him from where she wanted him most, she arched into his touch.

For a few fleeting seconds, whispers from the past invaded her mind. *What if something goes wrong?*

No. This wasn't six years ago. This was different.

As he grazed his fingers over her, Philippa's worries dissolved, and she reveled in what Dominic freely gave to her. Pure ecstasy. It grew stronger with every stroke over her center and soft flick of his tongue over her nipple.

She climaxed and he captured her cries in a kiss.

They removed their clothing, and Dominic sheathed himself in protection.

As he glided inside of her, they both shook from the power of need.

He rolled his hips and she joined him in a familiar rhythm of pleasure. One where they inherently knew what would make the other moan, grasp tighter and tremble as they fought to control what they couldn't stop. Tumbling over the edge and free-falling into bliss.

Chapter Ten

As Philippa snuggled closer to his chest, Dominic tightened his arm around her and smiled into the predawn darkness.

She'd stayed with him...

Last night, while she was in the shower, he'd come up with plenty of reasons for her not to leave. But when she'd come out of the bathroom, she'd snagged his burgundy shirt from the floor, set the alarm on her phone, and put it on the nightstand. Then she'd asked for something to tie her hair up with. He'd found a clean black bandana he sometimes wore in the restaurant kitchen. Once she tied up her hair, she'd crawled in bed beside him and promptly fallen asleep in his arms.

Unable to resist, Dominic pressed a soft lingering kiss to the top of her head. He could spend the entire day just holding her.

His phone dinged in a text. He eased partway from Philippa, reached beside him and quickly snagged it from the nightstand. It was Bailey.

Calling you.

It was four thirty in the morning. When Bailey had said she was calling first thing, he'd thought she'd meant at least seven his time. And why wasn't she asleep? It was one thirty in the morning in California.

Using one hand, he texted her back.

Talk later?

A text bubble with dots appeared.

Calling you now. It's urgent. Pick up!

Was she actually shouting at him in a text?

Careful not to wake Philippa, he got out of bed and found a pair of sweatpants in the dresser. Just as he pulled them on, his phone buzzed in Bailey's call.

Dominic snagged the black shirt he'd loaned Philippa last night from just under the bed before he slipped out the room.

He answered the call as he shut the door behind him. "Is whatever you have to tell me really that urgent it couldn't wait a few more hours?"

"Seriously? You woke me up at four in the morning just a week ago. No, it couldn't wait. I have good news. It's still on the bubble, so don't mention this to anyone, but the producers of the *Best Chef Wins* franchise want us to participate in a two-part crossover event. A reunion show with you and the rest of the *Best Chef Wins Los Angeles* cast from five years ago, followed by a special reunion episode on *Dinner with Dominic*."

Good news? Reliving his *Best Chef Wins Los Angeles* days—definitely not on his version of that list. This conversation required a clear head. He needed caffeine.

Working from memory, Dominic walked down the hall in the dark. He headed for the kitchen as he slipped on his shirt.

"Hello." Bailey called out. "Did I lose you?"

"No. I'm here. Why are the producers not cutting this deal with the winner? I was the runner-up."

"The winner doesn't have his own hit show and his restaurant closed two years ago. And according to my sources, *Best Chef Wins* needs a ratings boost."

As Bailey outlined what the collaboration would do for the *Best Chef Wins* franchise and *Dinner with*

Dominic, he set up the coffee maker with a brew pod and a black Flame & Frost embossed mug.

"Let me guess," he said. "The publicity firm thinks getting involved with this will be good for my brand."

"You say that like it's a bad thing."

"You know how I feel about my experience on that show."

"Yes, but this time, you're calling the shots, and they only want to highlight your strengths. You're known for really connecting with your guests, and that's what they're looking for with these episodes."

"They want drama. *Best Chef Wins* is a reality show. What's the catch?"

"There isn't one. It's a straightforward agreement. Part one would air as a network episode for *Best Chef Wins*. A look back at the past, visit the set type of thing. Part two would air on your show with you interviewing each of your fellow contestants while they prepare their signature dishes. At the end, all of you will share a meal celebrating the five-year anniversary of the season."

That sounded too easy. "Are you sure they don't want anything else?"

"The only request they may have is for you to spend a little more time talking with Destiny since the two of you were in a relationship."

And there was the catch—he knew there had to be one.

"There was no relationship between us. The producers of the show spun it that way."

"But the two of you did date each other."

"We weren't dating. We went out a few times *after* the show ended."

Two years ago, Destiny had come into the restaurant. She had found popularity through her single-girl-life themed vlog and hanging out with other reality show stars famous for being famous. She'd claimed she had a publishing deal in the works to write a cookbook and had asked for his help. Going for coffee had evolved into brainstorming sessions over dinner and her attending a couple of events with him.

But the chemistry hadn't been there. Not like it was with him and Philippa.

"You can't change fan perceptions about what they think happened on or after the show," Bailey insisted. "Your season of *Best Chef Wins* had been over for three years when you started seeing her, and fans of the show were still thrilled about Des and Dom."

Des and Dom—he hated the nickname the press had given them and the pure insanity that had come with it. Once their season of the show had aired, every time he'd walked out the door, there was someone sticking a camera in his face asking him questions about his supposed relationship with Destiny.

When they'd started seeing each other two years ago, it had started all over again. Members of the paparazzi had camped out in front of their homes and his restaurant. She'd craved the attention.

Remembering those moments set Dominic's teeth on edge. "If creating some story about Destiny and I is part of *Best Chef's* plans for a ratings boost, this conversation is over."

"It's not like the two of you would have to start dating again. Maybe a dinner or two before the show airs to create some curiosity, that's all."

"No."

"But this could kill the deal."

"My show isn't the one that needs the ratings boost."

During the silence, Dominic removed the full mug of coffee from the maker and took a sip. "You still there?"

"Yes. I just needed a minute to bang my head on the desk. Fine. I will insist they include in your contract that you and Destiny are not a package deal."

"Not so fast. What about the schedule? When do they want to start taping?"

"In three months, if they can get all the contracts signed in the next couple of weeks. The shows would air in late fall. Perfect timing with the opening of the Atlanta restaurant."

Bailey saw perfect timing. He saw a scheduling

disaster that wouldn't allow him a break between taping episodes of his own show, running Frost & Flame LA, and planning the opening of Frost & Flame Atlanta.

His caffeine buzz started to wane and weariness kicked in.

But mentioning the tight schedule to Bailey would just earn him a pep talk he wasn't in the mood to hear. He'd tackle that issue another day. "Keep me in the loop."

"I will."

A hint of light peeked through the blinds covering the windows in the living room. His schedule wasn't perfect, but his morning was, so far. Philippa was down the hall, and he didn't have to hide how he felt about her.

"Hey, what did you think of the cocktail mixers?" Bailey asked. "Are we doing business with the company?"

The image of Philippa, sleeping in his bed interrupted Dominic's response. He wanted a moment to just be with her before they had to jump into their day. He could wake her up with a cup of hazelnut-flavored coffee.

But hashing out a few details with Bailey about the contract for the mixers wouldn't take long.

Feeling lighter about the future, Dominic took another cup from the cabinet. "I haven't made up my mind yet. I have questions…"

* * *

Philippa bolted upright on the mattress and gasped for air, her mind still reeling from the bad dream. Her heart knocked harder against her rib cage as she looked around the unfamiliar room. The pieces fell into place.

I'm okay. I'm safe... She was in the spare bedroom at the guest cottage at Tillbridge. She'd spent the night with Dominic.

A shudder ran through her as she remembered the weird nightmare. She'd been in a restaurant kitchen, cooking eggs, but instead of her chef's uniform, she'd been wearing a purple sleepshirt.

Suddenly, the gray tiles had turned into quicksand, sucking her down. She couldn't cry out, and no one noticed she was in trouble. They'd kept doing their job as the floor had slowly entombed her in darkness.

The same stuck, smothering sensation that had come over her in the dream gripped Philippa now. Needing to move, she untangled her legs from the covers and sat on the edge of the bed.

Twilight turned the room a shadowy bluish gray.

She caught a glimpse of her wide-eyed reflection in the dresser against the wall. As she recalled the dream, the memory of the purple sleepshirt hovered in her thoughts.

The door opened.

"You're awake." Smiling, Dominic walked in carrying a steaming mug. "I'd hoped you wouldn't be."

Philippa pushed aside the nightmare and smiled back. "Why?"

"I had plans." Dominic leaned down and kissed her neck.

She breathed him in along with the scent of... *hazelnut coffee*... "Mmm, is that for me?"

"It is." He handed her the cup and sat beside her as she took a sip of the perfectly sweetened brew.

The warmth spreading inside of her chased away an inner chill leftover from the nightmare. "Thank you."

"You're welcome." Dominic slid an arm around her.

She leaned into him, and for a long moment they sat in companionable silence.

He pressed his lips to her temple and held her a bit closer. "I guess last night changes things?"

The uncertainty in his voice made her glance over at him. But what did she expect? Six years ago, she'd let him believe they'd just had a three-month fling, nothing special.

"It does." Philippa laid her hand on his thigh. "We can't claim that we're just colleagues anymore. What's our story now?"

"I think we need more time to figure that out." Laying his hand over hers, he intertwined their fingers. "We don't have to rush to explain our situation to anyone. We just have to take measures to keep our personal life private."

"So, what's the plan? Are we leaving our windows open so we can sneak in and out of each other's bedrooms?" She laughed but Dominic didn't. Her humor dissipated. "Oh."

His expression grew serious. "The guards outside the cottage have signed nondisclosure agreements, but the NDA is slanted toward protecting me. I'll have new ones drawn up that cover you, too. I'm also replacing the guards with ones from an LA-based firm we use whenever we need them. They work mainly with public figures and value discretion as part of their reputation."

For a few long seconds, Philippa remained speechless. She hadn't envisioned spending the night with him becoming a major privacy issue. "Okay...if that's best."

"I know. It's a lot. You normally don't have to think this way. If you'd rather not get involved with me because it's more than you bargained for, I'll understand." He gave a small smile that didn't reach his eyes.

Their situation had become more intense than she could handle with just one cup of coffee. But she was already involved. She couldn't wind the clock back and pretend she didn't care about him. "I do want to spend time with you while you're here. Can we take it one day at a time?"

Dominic's shoulders relaxed and he exhaled as if he'd been holding a pent-up breath. "We can definitely do that." As he leaned in, his gaze held hers. "But just so you know, I plan on taking advantage of every minute, you're willing to give me."

"I like the sound of that."

Closing the distance, she pressed her mouth to his.

Dominic cupped her cheek, and as the kiss deepened, he started to lean her back on the mattress.

The heat of the mug in Philippa's hand and the room growing a bit brighter made her hesitate. She spoke against his lips. "I would love for you to take advantage of me now, but I have to go home and get ready for work."

He eased back. "Work… I guess we do have to do that today. And you should probably leave before things get too active around Tillbridge."

Tillbridge…the staff. Always being careful. Keeping secrets. That's what they'd face over the next few weeks. As she handed him the coffee cup, his eyes reflected the same resignation she felt. What was she getting herself into?

But as daunting as it seemed, she didn't want to give up what they'd shared last night. She hadn't felt this level of anticipation and desire or been able to just let go like that with a guy in…six years.

A short time later, she stood with Dominic in the back entryway. She wore the burgundy shirt and held her damp one in her hand. "I'll see you later." They were meeting that afternoon with Rachel and Zurie at the outdoor arena where the screening event was taking place.

"See you then." When she turned to walk away, Dominic caught her hand, and she let him pull her back to him for a long goodbye kiss.

As Philippa left the driveway headed for home, happiness made her smile into the sun rising just over the horizon.

Farther down the road, horses grazed in the pasture to her right, and one of the staff from the stable worked near the run-in, an open wood shelter on the far side of the field.

The employees at the stable arrived long before sunup. On a Sunday, a few of the staff at Tillbridge, including the ones at Pasture Lane, would have started work nearly a half hour ago at five thirty.

Still, a flicker of apprehension over the possibility of being spotted close to the cottage tempted her to push down on the accelerator.

Stop being paranoid... She had the road to herself. And even if someone did see her, it wasn't like she was driving around with a flashing sign telling everyone where she'd just came from.

The red light blinked on the gas indicator.

Crap. She'd planned on getting gas yesterday after work.

The white-and-red sign for the Bolan Quick Stop

and Shop shone up ahead. Philippa made a left into the entrance and pulled up next to a free gas pump. After grabbing her debit card from her wallet, she got out and swiped it through the card reader.

As she pumped gas, diesel fumes from tractor trailers rolling slowly from the rear parking lot to the exit swarmed in the breeze.

Customers walking out of the store carrying coffee and giant cinnamon-roll breakfast sandwiches snagged her attention.

She'd heard the owner of the establishment, one of the mayor's cousins, had installed kitchen equipment in the back room to make them fresh.

At one time, Pasture Lane had served breakfast sandwiches from the restaurant's food van at the stable. But despite their popularity, they didn't make enough revenue to justify being open there in the morning. For sentimental reasons, she'd resisted making the decision to end serving breakfast using the van. The lime green vehicle had been her first food enterprise at Tillbridge before Pasture Lane Restaurant had been built almost five years ago.

The gas nozzle clicked, indicating the tank was full. She put it back on the pump, closed up her tank and pressed the yes button for a receipt on the transaction screen. Nothing came out of the slot.

Recently, overcharges on credit and debit cards at places like the Bolan Quick Stop and Shop had become an issue in the area. An interview with the police chief in the *Bolan Town Talk* had advised everyone to hold on to their receipts from the convenience stores as a precaution.

Philippa glanced down at Dominic's shirt, her pants and her tennis shoes. Not exactly fashionable, and the shirt obviously wasn't hers, but she was just running in for a receipt.

Inside the store, a combination of sunlight and bright fluorescents illuminated the aisles filled with grocery and toiletry items, and a wide array of junk food.

An endcap featured Maryland T-shirts, shot glasses, and other tourist souvenirs. At the rear of the store, a bulb on the verge of going out blinked in one of the beverage refrigerators lining the wall.

Cinnamon and the overly sweet smell of multiple flavored coffees brewing in the large coffee makers on the side wall hovered in the air.

She joined the line behind the only two other customers in the store. The man being checked out at the counter by a tired, bored-looking, college-aged girl counted out coins from a sock to buy scratch-off tickets.

The dark-haired woman directly in front of Philippa sighed and muttered, "This is taking forever."

And from the looks of things—the man had switched from counting out quarters to pennies—it wasn't ending anytime soon.

Not in a hurry, Philippa weighed her options. She had time to grab an orange juice. And maybe she'd check out the cinnamon roll sandwiches in the glass case near the coffee.

The Bolan Quick Stop and Shop wasn't serving restaurant-quality meals like Pasture Lane, but it was still smart to keep an eye on any operation, large or small, that served food in the area. Especially since they were all vying for local dollars.

Philippa got out of line. As she walked down one of the narrow, center aisles toward the beverage refrigerator, a row of small, blue-and-white rectangular boxes on the shelf caught her eye. Her steps faltered.

An urge she couldn't control made her reach toward the shelf as memories of the nightmare that had awakened her at the bungalow flooded into her mind. They faded into a recollection of her wearing faded blue leggings and her favorite purple sleep shirt under her winter coat. She'd dragged herself out of bed and gone to the drugstore for flu medicine, but then—

"Philippa?" Dominic strode toward her from the end of the aisle.

Startled, she jerked her hand back and knocked some of the pregnancy tests off the shelf.

She quickly bent down and gathered them from the floor, but she dropped one.

Dominic picked it up.

As he put it on the shelf, Philippa remained frozen for a moment. "What are you doing here?"

He held up her phone. "You forgot this on the nightstand. The security guard knew which way you were headed, so he pointed me this direction. I recognized your car at the pump." His gaze flickered to the pregnancy tests in her hand. "Are you okay?"

Still reconciling her memory with the dream, she struggled to answer.

"I'm fine." Philippa stuck the tests on the shelf, and then she took her phone. "Thank you. I should pay for my gas." Unable to meet his gaze, she slipped past him and went to the register.

Before Dominic left the store, he stopped beside her. "I'll meet you outside."

Still trapped in what she'd just recalled from her past, Philippa went through the motions of paying the cashier.

She'd never really forgotten about what happened back then. She'd just banished the memories to a place so deep in her mind, it had felt that way. But the confusion and sadness hitting her now struck almost as painfully as they had back then.

Outside, he stood near the driver-side door of her car.

Philippa paused in front of him. "Dominic... I..." How could she explain?

Grimness and concern shadowed his unwavering gaze. "Whatever it is. It doesn't change how I feel about you. Just tell me the truth."

Chapter Eleven

Dominic drove his black SUV rental behind Philippa's car down the narrow, two-lane road.

Their conversation outside the quick mart ten minutes earlier played through his mind.

Just tell me the truth...

I will...but not here.

Assumptions about what she'd say twisted knots in his gut. The worst-case scenario of Philippa planning to trap him into a pregnancy didn't sit right as a possibility. That left only one logical reason why she would need a pregnancy test. Philippa was possibly already pregnant. If she was, who was the father? Someone local? Was he still in her life?

Philippa turned left onto a long, paved driveway.

Yards away sat a white house with gray trim and shutters nestled in the trees.

Instead of driving toward the side-facing garage, Philippa kept going straight, past the house.

A smaller version of it with gray shutters on the front windows, a single-door garage and a porch surrounded by a white railing came into view.

She parked outside the garage, and he pulled in behind her.

They both got out of their cars, and Dominic followed her up the stairs to the wide porch.

She pointed to a grouping of wicker furniture with aqua cushions off to the side. "Do you mind if we sit out here?"

"This is fine with me."

"Good." She perched on the edge of the bench seat.

Signs of a fragile unease he'd never spotted in Philippa before made him want to pull her back up to her feet and hold her.

Dominic tamped down the urge and sat in the chair beside her.

He'd meant what he'd said earlier. Whatever she had to say wouldn't change the way he felt about her. It would impact their relationship moving forward. But he was there for her, even if she needed him as just a friend.

Dominic spoke first. "I don't care if you're pregnant. I just need to know if you're still with him."

"What?" Her eyes popped wide. "I'm not pregnant."

"But you were looking at pregnancy tests."

Philippa looked down for a long moment. "I'm not pregnant now...but I was six years ago when I left Coral Cove."

Her confession stunned him into silence.

She rushed on. "But I didn't know until three weeks after I left. I was in DC by then, living with a roommate. One day, we both were home, sick with the flu, and we ran out of medicine. I walked to the store up the street, and when I was there, I noticed the pregnancy tests, and it hit me. I was late. I grabbed one along with the medicine. But I didn't get a chance to use it. When I got home, I passed out."

Going to the store on her own even though she was sick. He could easily imagine her doing that. "Did someone take you to a hospital?"

"Yes. I was weak from dehydration." She looked up at him. "A nurse asked if I could be pregnant. Between the stress of moving to DC and being too sick to keep down my birth control pills, I didn't know. They did a blood test."

Philippa stood and walked to the porch railing. As she leaned her hands on it, she stared out at the trees.

An image flashed through his mind of the two of them on a secluded area of beach at Coral Cove.

While they'd watched the sunrise, one heated kiss had led them into doing more without a condom.

They weren't too concerned about the slipup. He and Philippa had been tested before the interview audition, and they were both disease-free. And she was on the pill. They'd used condoms as an extra precaution...except that one time.

Hope and concern hit him all at once. Did they have a child? Dominic got up.

Just as he went to ask, she met his gaze, and the bleakness he saw in her eyes made his chest ache. "What happened?"

She swallowed hard. "A week later, I started cramping and then..."

Not enough words existed to express what he wanted to say to her. He grasped her hand and squeezed. "I'm sorry. I should have been with you. I called, but when you didn't answer, I gave up. I should have tried harder to reach you."

"No. Us not communicating with each other— that's on me." Philippa squeezed back. "The day you called was when I found out I was pregnant, but I didn't know how to tell you. You were at Coral Cove. I'd just moved to DC. A baby would have completely changed our futures. And afterward... I was dealing with so much. Telling you then would have just made it harder for me to get through it."

Needing her close, he tugged Philippa toward

him. As they held each other, he breathed against the heaviness in his chest.

If she would have answered her phone that day and told him she was pregnant, there wouldn't have been a debate over what he would do. He would have chosen Philippa and their child. And if that would have meant giving up Coral Cove, he would have done it and not looked back.

And the loss…he would have done whatever he could to help her through it.

Dominic held her tighter. It hurt like hell to know she had borne the pain on her own for something he'd been a part of. From her reaction that morning at the mini mart, it still affected her.

He leaned back to look at her. "This morning, did seeing the pregnancy tests in the store trigger something?"

"Not on its own." Philippa's gaze dropped to her hands as she rested them on his chest. "I had a nightmare last night. In my dream, I was wearing the same purple sleep shirt I had on when it… when I…"

His heart ached for her as she blinked as if holding back tears.

"All these years later, I don't know why I'm not better at dealing with it." She shook her head. "I was just a few weeks along. It wasn't like I had to make any decisions or changes. Think about it. If my roommate and I hadn't run out of medicine that day, I might not have realized I was pregnant. I might have just thought I was having a heavier cycle than usual because I hadn't been taking my pills on a regular basis."

If only she hadn't—? Is that what she'd been telling herself all these years to cope with what had happened to her?

He cupped her cheek. "But you did know. You went through a difficult situation, and it came up for you now in an unexpected way. You're allowed to feel whatever you need to process it."

"But I didn't think I could still feel what I felt back then. The panic over what I was going to do. The fear that I wasn't ready. And when it came to an end, I was sad, but a part of me was also…relieved." She closed her eyes for a moment and tears leaked out. "I would have been responsible for helping that tiny being find its place in the world, but I had no idea where I was going or what I wanted for myself. Do you hate me for that?"

"No. Never." He dropped to eye level and cupped her face. "But you can't keep judging yourself for thinking that way. Being honest with yourself is a strength not a weakness."

A red van came up the driveway.

"That's Charlotte, my landlady." Philippa stepped away from him and faced the house. She swiped tears from her cheeks.

The van with Buttons & Lace Boutique in gold script on the side pulled up behind his rental.

An older woman with a silvery-blond bob, wearing blue leggings, flats and an oversized pink blouse stepped out of the driver side.

Charlotte left the engine running and stood by the car. "Hey, Philippa." She waved. "How are you?"

"I'm fine." Philippa waved back. "Are you on your way to the shop?"

"Yes. I have some inventory to take care of." A youthful glow of excitement lit up Charlotte's face. "You and Rina have to stop by and check out my new shoe section. There's a pair of sandals with your name on them. How's the water heater? Any more problems?"

"No, it's heating up fine. Thank you."

"Glad to hear it." Charlotte's gaze landed on Dominic. "Hello."

As she studied him, her genuine smile made it easier for Dominic to prompt his mouth to curve upward. "Hello."

"Well, I better get going. Let me know if you need anything." Charlotte got into the van. As she reversed out of the driveway, she waved again, and drove back toward the larger house.

Philippa laughed quietly as she returned Charlotte's wave.

"What's so funny?" he asked.

"The water heater was fixed last month."

"So she was being nosy? From the look on her face, I'm assuming she knows who I am? Does this mean by noon the whole town will know I was here?"

"Not so much nosy as being protective of me, and yes, she does know who you are. I saw one of your cookbooks in her kitchen. But Charlotte Henry is definitely not a gossip. She made Chloe's wedding dress and took care of the bridesmaids' dresses and not a word of it got out. She's like a vault."

Usually people who were great at keeping secrets had a few of their own. Maybe that's why Charlotte was so good at it. But the important thing was that Philippa trusted her. And it was good to know that the older woman cared about her. But he did, too. Did Philippa realize that?

Dominic took hold of Philippa's hand, and she turned to face him. The tears were gone, but hints of the emotional toll of their conversation showed on her face. "Do you have to go in to Tillbridge today? If not, I can cover for you at the meeting this afternoon with Rachel. You can take the day off."

"The screening party is only weeks away and we have a lot to do. I'm a part of it, and I'm going to pull my weight." Philippa laid her hand near his shoulder "I have the morning off. That's enough of a break. Don't worry about me. I'm fine."

But the urge to look after her was too close to the

surface. He hadn't been there when she'd needed him the most, and there was no way for him to make up for failing her back then. But from this point on, while he was with Philippa, her peace of mind, her needs, were his priority.

Dominic kissed her forehead. "I don't doubt that you can't handle anything, but I'm here for you, in any way you want me to be. Just tell me what you need."

Philippa stopped at the traffic light on the street bordering downtown Bolan.

A little over a couple of hours ago, after reassuring Dominic that she was fine, he'd left her house. She'd gotten some chores in before getting ready for work. With plenty of time on her hands, she'd taken a detour into town.

Just before she'd backed out of the driveway, Dominic had sent her a text, asking if she was okay.

Once again, she'd told him she was fine, and for the most part, she was. Telling Dominic everything had been hard. Reliving the moment in her mind had been harder. But she didn't regret talking about it with him.

Philippa made the turn onto Main Street.

At nine on a Sunday, people leisurely strolled the square, an area in the middle of town with neatly cut grass, flowering bushes and old-fashioned-styled streetlamps lining the paths. Sun glistened off the water cascading down the stone-fountain center-piece surrounded by park benches.

Other pedestrians window-shopped Buttons & Lace Boutique, the floral shop across the street and the Bolan Book Attic, the bookstore in town. They would open along with the other small businesses linked together in strip-mall fashion later that morning.

But on the corner farther down, a steady stream of customers entered and exited Brewed Haven. The stand-alone, two-story, light-colored brick building with large storefront windows was known for its pies, delicious pastries and other desserts and was the go-to place for coffee. The restaurant was also the weekend hot spot for meals throughout the day.

Philippa spotted a space in front of the flower shop and parallel parked. Leaving her chef's jacket in the car, she got out and walked up the street toward Brewed Haven. Instead of her Birkenstocks, she'd put on her black steel-toed boots with lime-green laces that morning.

Halfway there she passed the bookstore.

A poster featuring Dominic, advertising his upcoming book signing along with his book sat in the window.

Just tell me what you need...

He'd looked so sincere and concerned when he'd told her that. Was there something she didn't have before she'd told him everything that he could give her now? She didn't have an answer to that question, along with the others taking up residence in her mind. Talking with Rina would help. But first, she had to tell Rina what had happened with Dominic six years ago.

Would Rina understand she hadn't avoided telling her? That she'd just trained herself not to think about certain parts of her past? Lately, she'd teased Rina about her "eminent" future of having enough kids with Scott to fill an entire sports team roster. Now that her memories had resurfaced, would it feel awkward to laugh and tease Rina about it?

And what about her current relationship with Dominic? He'd said how he felt about her wouldn't change, and she believed that. But before he'd left, she'd sensed a shift in him. Maybe the shock over what she'd told him had settled in. He'd mentioned she had a right to process her feelings, but he did, too.

At the corner opposite Brewed Haven, Philippa crossed the street, and as she drew closer to the cafe, the scent of freshly brewed coffee wafted in the air.

She opened the glass door and walked inside.

A short line of people waited at the curved station. Baristas wearing jeans and purple T-shirts with the cafe's yellow coffee cup logo filled orders for drinks and grabbed pastries for customers from the glass case underneath the counter.

On the right, a sprinkling of customers sat in the

purple booths lined along the wall and at the light wood tables with purple-and-yellow floral center-pieces, enjoying brunch.

The sound of familiar, happy laughter drew Philippa's attention to the smaller alcove on the opposite side of the cafe, where more customers sat at round tables or on the beige couches deco-rated with purple throw pillows tucked under the side windows.

Rina, dressed similarly to her staff and wear-ing a yellow apron chatted with a dark-haired man at one of the tables. He pointed to his open laptop in front of him, and she nodded in agreement to what he said.

Not wanting to interrupt, Philippa stepped for-ward to join the coffee line.

"Hey, Philippa." Mace Calderone tapped her arm.

"Hi, Mace." Philippa took in his beige-and-brown deputy sheriff's uniform. "Taking a coffee break?"

The tan-skinned, dark-haired deputy smiled. "Yeah, I got a long one ahead of me. Plus, I was up early this morning. Zurie wanted to go over the secu-rity plan for the movie screening. She said you guys have a meeting with the planner this afternoon?"

"Yes. We're going over the kitchen-trailer setup at the arena with Dominic and his team."

"Dominic's a busy man. Before I met with Zurie this morning, I dropped by to check in with the se-curity people at the cottage. They said he was out."

Did he know she'd stayed at the cottage or that Dominic had left the cottage that morning to find her? Or was she reading too much into Mace's steady gaze. "He has a lot on his plate with the screening and taping episodes of his show here."

Mace tipped his head with a nod. "I'm sure he does."

"What is this? A family reunion?" Rina nudged Mace's arm, then gave Philippa a tight hug. "You didn't tell me you were coming by."

Philippa returned the embrace. "It's my morning off. Jeremy and Quinn are taking care of brunch."

"Lucky girl, you could have slept in." Rina slumped her shoulders in mock exhaustion. "I haven't done that in weeks. I hope the reason you're here was worth giving that up."

"I wanted to talk to you about something."

"Next customer, please," the barista called out.

Philippa was next. She stepped out of line. "Mace, you go ahead."

"You sure?"

"Yes. You know how it is. I have to grab Rina while I can catch her."

"True." Smiling, he headed for the counter. "I'll see you two later."

Rina poked her. "You know I'm never too busy for you. Do you want to eat? There isn't a waiting list yet. We can sit in the dining area."

"Can we talk in your office?" Customers walked

in for coffee, and Philippa and Rina scooted more to the side. "It's private."

"Okay. Then, we should probably walk and talk, so there won't be any interruptions. Hold on. I'll let Darby know I'm stepping out. And I'll grab us some coffee."

A few minutes later, full cups in hand, they walked down the street toward the square.

As they passed by Buttons & Lace, Rina gripped her arm. "I heard Charlotte expanded her shoe section. Did you know?"

"I found out from her when she came by the house this morning. She said we have to stop by."

"Has Charlotte eased up on acting like a mother hen?"

When Philippa had first moved in, Charlotte had checked in on her almost every day. "A little. She just wants to make sure I'm comfortable."

Rina looped her arm through Philippa's. "I still think you should have moved into my spare room."

"And spend my time night gardening with you and making friends with the raccoons? No, thank you."

"It wouldn't have been that bad."

"Oh, yes it would have. And as much as Scott likes me, I think he would prefer to be the only one night gardening with you."

"Yeah, and he's really good at it." Mischievous humor beamed in Rina's face.

Philippa couldn't hold back a laugh. Leave it to Rina to put her in a good mood.

They crossed the street, then settled on a bench near the water fountain. In companionable silence, they people watched and drank their coffees.

As Philippa sipped the hazelnut-flavored brew in her cup, she thought of the coffee Dominic had brought her that morning. She turned toward Rina. "Dominic and I slept together last night."

Rina stared at her with a neutral expression. "Well…okay."

"I tell you I've slept with my ex, and that's all you can say?"

"Until you say more, I'm not sure if that's a good thing or a bad thing."

Philippa looked from Rina to the fountain. In true best-friend fashion, Rina had managed to encapsulate what was really on her mind. "Last night, it was a good thing. This morning was…tough."

"Oh, no. Were you two pretending to have a casual, non-awkward conversation when you first woke up?"

"No, actually he brought me hazelnut coffee."

"He remembered that's your favorite?" Smiling, Rina turned to face Philippa. "What happened after that?"

Like ripping off a Band-Aid, there was no easy way through it. "I left. Stopped for gas at the Bolan Quick Stop and Shop, and started looking at pregnancy tests on the shelf. And that's where Dominic found me when he came in to give me my phone."

Rina mouth dropped open. "Tell me that didn't happen."

"It did."

"But why were you looking at pregnancy tests? Was there a problem with the protection he used?"

"No, the condoms worked just fine."

"Plural, condoms. Okay, busy night. But you're still on birth control, right? Sure, a pregnancy can still happen but it's rare, like in the single digits."

"It is." Philippa paused to gather her words. "But it happened to me six years ago…with Dominic."

Taking advantage of Rina's stunned silence, Philippa told her about what had happened back then and what occurred that morning.

Rina laid her hand on Philippa's arm. Empathy filled her face. "I'm so sorry. I can't imagine all that you went through."

Philippa almost brushed Rina's caring aside, but what Dominic had said about her being allowed to feel whatever she needed to process it, even after all these years, came to mind. "It wasn't easy. I struggled for a while. But landing at Tillbridge, meeting you and then getting to know you better when I took over the food van. It all helped."

"I'm so glad you found your way here." Eyes bright as if she was about to cry, Rina pulled Philippa into a big hug.

"I am, too." Philippa held her coffee cup out of the way and breathed against Rina's tightening hold. "Please, let me go."

"Never. You're my best friend. And, no matter what, I'm always here for you."

"No, really. Let me go. You're suffocating me."

"Oh, sorry." Rina released her.

Philippa took a huge breath. "Thank you. Aside from Dominic, you're the only person I've told."

"Are you glad you told him?"

"I am. In the moment, it wasn't easy, but now it feels like a weight has been lifted. Like telling him was the last thing I needed to do to put it behind me."

"How did he take it?"

"He was kind and supportive. And wanted me to tell him what I needed." Philippa paused, not quite sure what to say next. Dominic had been wonderful. Still, the way he'd acted right before he left felt off.

"But? And don't say nothing." Rina circled her finger in the air. "You've got that I'm-bothered-by-something look on your face. Just say it. He was kind, supportive and asked what you needed, but…"

"Before Dominic left, he kissed me on the forehead."

"He kissed you goodbye. What's the problem? You didn't want him to?"

"No, I did. But he's never kissed me on the forehead like that. Ever. It was like he was pitying me. I don't know." Philippa sunk against the back of the bench seat. "Maybe I'm judging him based on how I think he should act. I'm sure what I told him wasn't easy to hear. Just like me, he has a right to process what I told him in a way that's best for him."

"He does. But I'm wondering… He asked what you needed. What did you tell him?"

"I didn't give him an answer. I didn't have one."

Rina offered up a shrug. "Maybe he wasn't pitying you. He could be confused. For a guy, when the person they care about has been hurt or is hurting—their go-to is to try and fix something. But he can't fix the past and make it better for you. That's probably hard for him and rather than say or do the wrong thing, he's staying in the neutral zone."

Was Dominic confused, and that's what the kiss really reflected? Philippa took a sip of lukewarm coffee. "He's confused? I'm confused. I don't know what I need from him."

Rina sat back on the bench and sighed. "You wouldn't be the first to have felt that way. I hate to tell you, but you might not know what you need from him until you need it."

Chapter Twelve

Philippa sat beside Tristan in the golf cart as he reversed out of a space in the parking lot of the guesthouse, a two-story white building with green trim and a green pitched roof. At three in the afternoon on a Sunday, most of the guests had checked out at the end of brunch a half hour ago.

He sped across the lot toward the narrow-paved trail bisecting two fenced-in, grassy fields that comprised the north pasture. A breeze ruffled the ends of her hair, secured by a green headband. Her dark T-shirt and pants absorbed the rays of the sun, but the same breeze kept her cool.

A navy ball cap with the Tillbridge logo covered his short black hair and shielded Tristan's face,

which was a medium brown after hours in the sun.
His blue short-sleeved Tillbridge T-shirt and slightly
faded jeans had a few smudges of dirt on them, and
his boots had a layer of dust. Even though he was a
co-owner of the Tillbridge operation, the tall, lean
former bull rider was hands-on with his job of stable manager.

He glanced at Philippa. "Sorry I was late picking
you up. I hadn't planned on going to this meeting.
I was grooming horses when Zurie called and said
I had to take her place."

"You didn't have to come for me. I could have
driven." Uneven pavers jostled the cart and Philippa
held on to the edge of the seat.

"No. Driving yourself there would have been a
waste of gas. Besides, you can tell me about this
event planner we're meeting with. Zurie was a little
too happy to take care of a leak in one of the guest-
rooms and pass this task to me. From her tone, I'm
guessing she's had enough of—Rachel. Is that her
name?"

"Yes, that's it."

"You've been working with her. Is she that difficult?"

Still a tad annoyed by how Rachel had handled
replacing her with Dominic but not wanting to trash
her name, Philippa chose her words wisely. "Let's
just say you're probably on-target with your guess
about why Zurie wanted out of the meeting."

He chuckled. "Noted. The planner may be a pain, but Zurie's had nothing but good to say about Dominic and his team. I met him this morning. He came by with the location scout to talk about taping some general footage at the stable. Seems like a good man. He's not full of it like a few of the celebrities I've met while hanging with Chloe."

Since the filming of *Shadow Valley*, Chloe's notoriety had risen. Despite the pressure of fame, Tristan seemed to take it all in stride. But it hadn't been that way when the two first met. How long had it taken him to find his place in her life and career? Would she be able to do the same if she and Dominic remained together?

Philippa set the thought aside. She was getting ahead of herself. They were in new territory, as Rina had pointed out. A place where maybe they weren't meant to be a couple. Usually she didn't believe in fate, but the peace she'd started to feel after telling him everything that morning had only grown stronger.

Maybe Dominic showing up in her life again wasn't about them getting back together but about her finding true closure about what happened six years ago.

Tristan stopped near a metal pasture gate on the right. As he went to put the golf cart in Park, she stopped him. "I'll do it. What's the code?"

"One-two-two-eight. Thanks."

"You're welcome." Philippa got out, keyed in the code and swung the wide gate open.

As she waited for Tristan to drive through it, bittersweet acceptance hovered inside of her as she thought about things possibly coming to an end with Dominic. She breathed more of it in, along with the pungent mix of grass and horse manure.

Some people hated it, but to her, it smelled like a fresh start. Just like it had the very first day she'd arrived at Tillbridge.

After closing the gate, she got back into the golf cart, and Tristan drove toward the two-hundred-foot, sandstone-colored structure. It had been built to accommodate the needs of filming the movie. Now it was in the process of being transformed into a showpiece for the stable.

The state-of-the-art, temperature-controlled facility would not only house an arena large enough to train horses, but it would also be able to accommodate the needs of competitors training for rodeos and horse shows.

From what Rina had told her, the indoor arena was something Tristan had wanted for years.

"How is the renovation going?" she asked. "Last time I was here, they were painting the walls and installing the flooring."

"They finished most of it last week. They're working on that and the offices now." As Tristan maneuvered around a small hole in the grass, he pointed to the left of the building. "After the screening party is over, we'll start on the covered corridors that will lead to the outdoor arena and the new stable."

"Will you move the stable offices here?"

"I'm not sure. We're still considering it along with kicking things up a notch with more support for competitors—top trainers, specialized clinics for learning opportunities and hosting small events. Ideally, this would become one of the go-to places in the region."

Tristan parked in the front paved lot of the building, next to the four-seater golf cart Quinn, Jeremy, Eve and Teale had used to get to the arena. A red car was parked farther down, but she didn't see Dominic's rental. Had he hitched a ride with someone?

They got out of the cart, and Philippa walked ahead of Tristan down the sidewalk and through the glass-door entrance.

Cool air rushed over her as she stepped inside of the dark wood lobby with a reception desk to the right.

The impressive view of sophistication and practicality drew Philippa forward to the wide glass overlooking the main area.

A series of dark wood beams supported a white arched ceiling and two rows of translucent panels down the center of it. The beams continued down the wood walls that were in shades of light and warm brown wood. A dark wood ladder-railing fence surrounded the sand-covered area in the middle. Round, drop-down lights helped illuminate the space, and on the opposite end, a wide barn-style door sat partially open, letting in the sun.

Tristan joined her at the window. "They're up there, in the viewing box."

She followed where he pointed to the right. In the middle of bench-style bleachers along the wall was a room with a big window overlooking the arena.

Philippa caught a glimpse of Dominic, and happiness along with a small seed of anxiety tugged in her chest. Maybe the whole kiss on the forehead had just been a fluke reaction in the moment and she shouldn't read anything into it.

She followed Tristan through the door exiting the lobby. A walkway to the right, along the arena fence, took them past the wood bleachers. Instead of walking through the short tunnel to the wide corridor ahead, they went into a door on the left and up a short flight of stairs.

Tristan opened the door, and as she entered the wood-floored room with a sandstone fireplace, her gaze met Dominic's.

Something akin to sadness briefly flashed across his face before he looked back to the group. No. Not sadness. Was it pity or guilt? Her heart sank.

Rachel walked up to Tristan with a wide smile.

"Hello. We met a few months ago. I'm Rachel Everett."

"Tristan Tillbridge." He shook hands with the event planner.

Rachel looked to Philippa, and her smile dimmed. "Chef Gayle. You made it."

Before Philippa could respond, Dominic jumped in. "We appreciate you making time for this." His tone was formal and stilted as he looked to Philippa. "Especially since you have a lot on your plate today...like a busy schedule at Pasture Lane."

Teale and Eve exchanged perplexed looks, as if they'd missed something.

Quinn and Jeremy glanced at Philippa with slightly worried expressions.

Philippa answered him and her staff with a reassuring nod and a smile, "Everything's great at the restaurant and I'm excited to hear about the layout for the event."

Rachel took over the conversation, turning to the window and explaining how the sand in the arena would be covered with raised, temporary flooring.

A lot on my plate? They'd had an important conversation that morning. And yes, she'd cried, but she wasn't falling apart. She was fine. How many times did she have to tell him that? Philippa fought the urge to confront Dominic and tell him again. Not that she could if she wanted to—for some reason, he was keeping his distance from her.

As Rachel finished going over the seating arrangements, she turned back to the group. "Lighting is an issue. So we'll have to create it with candles in the centerpieces on the tables. They're going to be huge. Maybe we should just use big ol' candelabras." She released a breezy laugh. "But of course, I won't. That would be tacky. One thing we do have going for us are the skylights in the ceiling. Guess it breaks up the monotony for the people riding their horses in a circle."

Standing next to Philippa, Tristan crossed his arms over his chest. "They're not cosmetic. Natural light reduces the glare and shadows in the arena that could spook the horses."

"Right, the horses." Rachel flashed a bright smile. "And what about in here?" She opened her arms, encompassing the space. "Are there decorating plans for this room? This is where the stars of the film will meet with our largest donors before the event starts."

Tristan gave a nod. "Brown leather side chairs, a matching love seat and coffee table, plus stools in front of the window. They're arriving in two weeks. That's plenty of time before the event."

"Brown? That's so…rustic." Rachel's nose twitched with the same finicky expression she wore when she called Philippa's catering menu *decent*. "I'll make arrangements for something better to be brought in for the event."

"And what about our furniture?" Tristan asked.

Rachel focused on tapping info into her phone. "I suggest you get a PODS."

On the way down the corridor toward the back of the arena, Tristan murmured to Philippa, "Get a PODS. Is she for real? It's not like we don't have more important things on our task list besides changing out furniture she doesn't approve of just weeks ahead of the event."

"I know exactly how you feel."

He tapped a message into his phone. "Now I understand why Zurie bailed on this meeting. She probably suspected Rachel had demands. Zurie owes me."

Outside the barn-style door at the rear of the arena, the group discussion about the setup of the mobile kitchens, thankfully, didn't require as much input from Rachel. And they were all in agreement about the staging area for the servers and where they would enter and leave the arena.

Philippa made a note in her phone about service for VIPs in the viewing box. The kitchenette in the space wasn't outfitted to handle the small cocktail hour. Equipment would have to be brought in.

She stumbled.

Dominic suddenly appeared at her side and took her arm. "Careful. Are you good?"

Philippa gritted her teeth and resisted the urge to yell at him *I'm fine!* "Yes, thank you."

She marched away from him, more than ready to leave with Tristan.

Back at Pasture Lane, she grabbed the tablet they used for ordering out of her desk.

Dominic walked into her office. "Do you have a minute to talk about the portable kitchens?"

That was the last thing they needed to discuss, but the party, not their personal life came first. "If you can talk while I work. Sure."

She grabbed her zip-up, hooded blue sweatshirt from a hook behind the door and strode from the office.

Dominic followed her into the walk-in refrigerator, impervious to the cold in his short sleeves.

Philippa counted blocks of cheese on the metal shelf. "I'm listening."

"You're doing inventory. I could help. Do you want me to input the numbers while you count?"

Asking if he could assist her was a legitimate question. But under the present circumstances, it struck a nerve. "I can't do this. I won't do this." She left the tablet on the shelf and advanced on Dominic.

"Is there something wrong with the inventory?" he asked.

His honestly puzzled expression deflated some of her irritation. "No. But there's something going on with you. I realize finding out about the pregnancy this morning was a lot to take in. And just like you gave me permission to process how I felt about it, I respect that you need the same. But if you're feeling sorry for me or maybe guilty for not being there six years ago—don't."

Dominic opened his mouth as if to deny it, then paused. "That's not how I meant to make you feel. I'm just trying to…" He reached out to touch her. His hand and his shoulders fell with a long breath. "Maybe I do feel guilty. I just want you to know that I meant what I said about being here for you now."

"What I want you to know is that after telling you everything that happened, I feel like a burden was lifted from me that I didn't even realize I was carrying. You gave that to me. And I'm so grateful."

His brow lifted in surprise. "I did?"

"Yes." Philippa laid her hand on the middle of his chest. "And the last thing I want is for you to carry around guilt for whatever you think you did wrong." What she had to tell him next wasn't easy to say, but it had to be said. "As much as I want to be with you now, if guilt is all you feel when you look at me, we can't be together. But we can still work on this party as friends."

"No." Dominic laid his hand over hers, and his heart thumped against her palm. "I don't feel guilt when I look at you. From the moment I saw you again, all I've wanted is to be with you. And what you told me didn't change that. I was trying not to be selfish by putting my feelings first. I thought maybe you needed space or time away from me. I didn't know."

Rina was right. He *was* confused about what to do for her. She moved closer to him. "What I need… No, what I want is you."

"If that's what you want, you got me, Philippa. You always have." He intertwined his fingers with hers on his chest. "So where do we go from here?"

The outside handle on the walk-in door rattled and they moved apart.

Quinn opened the door and peeked inside. "Chef, we have a big problem."

"What's going on?" As Philippa rushed out of the refrigerator, Dominic was close behind.

"We're maxed out with reservations," Quinn said.

"And the waitlist is filling up," Bethany added, walking up next to Quinn. "And the front desk said people are hanging out in the lobby."

"That's odd." Philippa mentally ran through the event calendar in Bolan. Nothing stood out. "Did we miss a big event?"

"I asked the last person who called in for a reservation." Bethany's gaze slid to Dominic. "Someone spread a rumor that you're in the kitchen tonight."

"Where did that come from?" Philippa looked to Dominic.

He shrugged. "I don't know anything about it. If

publicity had planned something, they would have told me before now."

"Maybe it's not that bad," Quinn piped in with hopefulness in her tone. "Maybe the people in the lobby are just waiting to see Dominic for an autograph or a picture."

Bethany massaged her temples. Anxiety reflected in her flushed face. "The hungry masses are going to slaughter us."

Philippa silently agreed with Bethany. "I'll go to the lobby and let people know the rumor isn't true. As far as the incoming reservations, we'll just have to tell them the truth as well. People will be upset with us, but we just have to remind them, we didn't advertise he'd be here."

"They're not going to accept that as an excuse," Dominic spoke to Philippa. "There's only one way around this. They came here for food. Let's give it to them."

"No." She shook her head. "You haven't had time to prepare a menu, and you're not familiar with ours. I can't ask you to put yourself in a bad position."

"I won't be in a bad position if it's a collaborative effort. Pasture Lane is *your* restaurant. You and your staff know the menu inside and out. I'll just follow your lead."

"And in the front of the house, we could squeeze in extra tables to cut down the wait," Bethany said.

"And a few of the housekeeping and front desk staff have experience working in the restaurant. I could check in with their supervisors and see if they can spare them."

Philippa started to object, but what she saw in Dominic's eyes stopped her. He wasn't jumping in to help out of guilt that a rumor was spread about him being there. He genuinely wanted to do it, and he was up for a challenge. Back in the day, they were a good team on the front lines of the kitchen at Coral Cove. Did they still have it? If they were a little rusty, they could work out the kinks now instead of at the screening party.

Philippa swallowed the *no* to Dominic's offer that had been hovering on her lips. "Okay. Let's do this."

Chapter Thirteen

Dominic tied a black apron around his waist. Pasture Lane was opening in a few minutes, and they seemed ready.

Earlier he'd called Teale and Eve to see if they could help. Eve was busy, but Teale was available to assist, and Jeremy had come in with her. The two of them would monitor the orders coming in and the plates going out.

Dominic walked to the center cooking station in the kitchen, double-checked the burners and the grill in front of him, and made sure he had ample pans, oils and the seasonings he would need nearby.

He glanced toward the front of the kitchen where Philippa conferred with Zurie.

They'd already worked out a plan. He, Philippa and Quinn would handle the main entrées while the rest of the cooks took care of the side dishes.

Philippa joined him at the station a few feet over. She already had her game face on but gave him a quick smile as she adjusted the orders monitor attached to a rail above.

Determination settled inside of him. He wouldn't let her down. This was his chance to make up for being a bonehead. He'd realized after their talk in the walk-in, that when she'd cried on the porch at her house, he'd viewed it as her falling apart. And he'd assumed it was his job to pick up the pieces to make up for not being there for Philippa. He hadn't considered her sharing what happened would free her of something that was keeping her from being more of herself.

"First order up," Jeremy called out.

Dominic's focus kicked in as he read the order for pan-seared steak and grilled salmon on the monitor in front of him. "Firing steak."

"Firing salmon," Philippa said.

Although he wasn't in his own kitchen, as time passed, he quickly settled into the practiced rhythm of starting one order, moving on to the next and the next and then back again to plate up the finished products. Managing the hectic pace came as naturally to him as breathing. Innate and necessary. He needed the heat rising around him along with aro-

mas of impending perfection. And Philippa standing beside him made the moment even better.

Her joy. Her skill. Her eye for making good even
more wonderful. The confidence she'd gained over
the years as a leader in her own kitchen. It fueled
the adrenaline running through him. A ping of happiness and something Dominic had never felt before
swelled in his chest. She was…phenomenal. And
she was his again. At least temporarily.

Teale hurried over to him, carrying a plate with
a pan-seared steak, the most popular entrée of the
night. "A mistake was made on an order. We need
to kill this on the fly."

Dominic quickly put the steak in a pan and
tamped down judgment. There was no accounting
for taste. If the customer wanted it extremely well-
done, he'd give it to them.

As he handed a clean plate with the steak back
to Teale, a couple of flashes of red appeared on the
monitor in front of him, an indication that the maximum time it should take to complete some of the
orders was almost up. He glanced at Quinn's station.

She was falling behind.

"How much longer on the vegetarians for thirty-
nine and forty?" Jeremy asked.

"Ten out," Quinn responded.

That was way too long. He caught Philippa's eye.
From her concerned expression, she also realized

they were dangerously close to being in the weeds. "Can you handle this for minute?" she asked him.

"Got it." Focus on maximum, he dialed in, cooking her parts of the menu as well as his while she jumped over to help Quinn catch up.

"Eighty-six the baked potatoes," one of the cooks handling the sides called out.

They were out of baked potatoes already? *Damn.* Dominic slid perfectly grilled salmon from a spatula onto a plate. They were running low on a few items and were already at the point of stretching others. Would they make it?

After what seemed like forever and no time at all, Teale shouted. "Last order out. We're done."

Whoops erupted in the kitchen, and smiles became infectious.

Philippa's smile was the best of all.

He winked at her, and she laughed and fanned her face.

Cheers grew louder as the staff started to applaud him and Philippa. They both redirected the accolades back to the staff.

Bethany hurried over to him wearing a rosy-cheeked smile. "The mayor is here with a few of his family and friends. He's wondering if you could come out and say hello to everyone."

Dominic waved off the request. "This is Philippa's restaurant, not mine. I was just helping out."

And he wasn't taking credit for something that

shouldn't have happened in the first place. Things had worked out in Pasture Lane's favor, but it could have easily gone sideways. And more importantly, he wanted to finish his conversation with Philippa to make sure they were on the same page with their relationship.

"You should go out there." Philippa nudged him.

"No. This was a team effort."

"And right now, you're our star player, Chef Extraordinaire." With a bit of tease in her smile, she nudged his arm again. "You're up. And tonight, everybody wins. Go make people happy."

Make people happy. If he didn't go out there, people might leave unhappy. And that could reflect on Philippa and her people. After all the work they'd put in to make dinner a success, they deserved nothing but praise for their performance.

He spoke to Bethany, "Please tell them I'm on my way."

"Sweet." Bethany rushed back to the front of the house.

As he took off his apron, he looked at Philippa. "I won't be long. Can you wait for me?"

"I'm not going anywhere." He followed her gaze to the stacked dirty pans, utensils and food-splattered surfaces. "We're going to be here awhile."

In the dining room, he chatted, smiled and took pictures. When customers complimented him about the food, he gave credit where it was due—

to Philippa and her staff. But not everyone heard him. They were too enamored with the idea of him being their chef for the night.

Close to an hour later, he finally slipped back into the kitchen.

The cooking stations were already clean. Kitchen helpers scrubbed ovens and other equipment. A combination of staff members from Pasture Lane and departments in the guesthouse helped at the dish machine.

The door to Philippa's office was closed, and he glanced through the window.

Quinn sat in the gray chair in front of the desk. Philippa leaned back on the edge of the desk, facing Quinn as she talked to her. As Quinn looked down at her hands in her lap, Philippa patted the young woman's shoulder in a comforting gesture.

Quinn had looked rattled when she'd fallen behind during dinner. Was she upset about that?

Just as he started to walk away, the office door opened, and Quinn walked out.

Head down, she passed him but not before he saw her blotchy cheeks and the bleakness in her red-rimmed eyes.

Dominic went into Philippa's office. "Is Quinn alright?"

"She will be. She's embarrassed about falling behind on the line at dinner."

"Tonight was intense. It could have happened to any one of us."

"That's what I told her." Philippa released a sigh. "One of the things that tripped her up tonight was being intimidated. She doesn't see herself as good enough, but she is. And comparing herself to Jeremy isn't helping. I advised her to stop dwelling on what she sees as her faults and focus on the type of leader she wants to be in the kitchen. On the other hand, sometimes I wish Jeremy would push himself a little harder. They both have so much potential, they're just scratching the surface."

In that moment, he saw glimpses of Chef LeBlanc in her. "What you're noticing in Jeremy, Chef LeBlanc spotted in me. She told me I had a choice to make. I could stay comfortable where I was and just be a good sous chef and an okay head chef someday. Or I could reach for something more, risk falling flat on my ass and probably achieve something better than I ever expected."

"That definitely sounds like Chef LeBlanc." Philippa released a wry laugh. "She was good at sharing advice involving choices."

He leaned back on the edge of the desk beside her. "What did Chef LeBlanc tell you?"

Philippa's smile faded a little. "I'll tell you another time. You asked me to wait for you. I'm assuming you want an answer to the question you asked me in the walk-in?"

"I do."

She leaned in, bringing her shoulder close to his. "I still think we should take things a day at a time and just enjoy being with each other."

For the part of him that not only wanted her but also to gain an understanding of who she was now, what she was suggesting sounded too simple. But maybe that's what she wanted. Uncomplicated. And he'd respect her wishes, especially if it moved them to the enjoying part of their relationship a lot quicker. He just wanted to get back to holding her in his arms without any reservations between them.

Dominic bumped his shoulder against hers. "It's a deal."

Chapter Fourteen

Philippa sat at her desk, taking advantage of down-time after lunch to work on a draft of the food order for the party. It was massive, and they still had more menu items to decide on. But finishing the menu wouldn't take long since she and Dominic saw eye-to-eye on almost everything.

Her gaze drifted to the spot on the edge of the desk where they'd sat four days ago and agreed to keep seeing each other. Things had been good between them personally since then. And the planning for the event was falling right into place. But they could use a lot more couple's time outside of work.

His schedule had ramped up and his days were packed. He was running his LA restaurant long-distance and planning to open a new restaurant in Atlanta. Plus he was traveling to local farms and other places near Bolan to record segments that would be included in upcoming farm-to-fork themed episodes on his show. And on top of all that, he was still working out details for the screening party with her and their teams.

And now that the cottage was fully outfitted as a set kitchen, privacy there was almost nonexistent. It also served as workspace for the film crew and someone was always around. By the time he was alone, Dominic was tired. Their intimate moments, so far, had consisted of a few passionate kisses in the walk-in like the one they'd shared yesterday. He'd stopped by on his way to tape a segment at a family-owned operation that specialized in growing herbs for their line of preservative free seasonings.

It had been nice, and the kiss had added a spark to her morning, but she really missed him. And she was concerned about him not getting a break from work outside the few hours he slept.

"Earth to Philippa." Rina waved at her from the doorway.

"Hey. Why are you just standing there? Come in."

Rina shut the door behind her, then dropped into the gray chair. "I wasn't just standing there. I called your name twice, but you didn't hear me. I came to tell you that I changed your dessert order. You'd requested twelve rhubarb pies and two apple ones. I figured it was a mistake because I know you use more apple pies than that in a week, so I switched it around."

"I ordered twelve rhubarb pies? I must have been really distracted or something when I placed the order. Thanks for catching it."

"Does that 'distraction or something' have anything to do with the person who put that glow on your face?"

Philippa started to deny it, but as she thought of Dominic, she could feel happiness shimmering inside of her. "Is it that obvious?"

"Yes," Rina laughed. "They can probably see that glow from outer space."

"Great. I wonder what people are saying. I'm surprised Anna hasn't mentioned it in the *Town Talk*."

"If people are gossiping, I haven't heard about it. And all Anna talks about nowadays is the exclusive Dominic's people promised her at the party."

"That was the trade-off for her not pushing for a story about us at Coral Cove. I hope they know what they're doing. Backstage access. No limitations, and everyone in attendance is fair game for an interview if they're willing to give her one."

"Wow. No wonder she's keeping her mouth shut. But you smiling for no reason instead of frowning over work is worth talking about."

"Did I really frown that much before?"

Rina's good-natured expression came with a small shrug. "You were preoccupied with running this place, so it was understandable. But I'm also happy something else is also on your mind. I want details."

"There are none." Philippa sat back in the chair and explained the situation between her and Dominic.

When she finished, Rina slowly nodded. "Sounds familiar. The struggle for quality time together pretty much comes with the territory of being with someone connected to the entertainment industry. Tristan has experienced it with Chloe, and I have, too, with Scott."

"Any suggestions besides being understanding about Dominic's career? And I already mentioned to him about trying to spend more time together."

"When Scott's been working full-on for weeks, he forgets the benefits of slowing down for a few days. So I give him a few helpful reminders about what he's missing."

From the gleam in Rina's eyes, it was easy to imagine the theme of those helpful reminders.

Philippa laughed. "I'll keep that suggestion in mind."

The conversation switched to the screening party.

"I have news." Rina leaned in. "Scott called me

this morning. He is going to make it back in time for the party. I'm so excited."

Tillbridge Horse Stable and Guesthouse was one of the major donors buying a table for the event, plus they'd contributed directly to Holland's scholarship fund.

"That's great. Do you know what you're wearing?"

"I'm still debating. Chloe said the dress code is on the formal side of dressy casual. A nice cocktail dress would probably work."

"Or a jumpsuit."

Rina's brow raised with interest. "I hadn't thought of that. Something that skews toward elegance. I'll stop by Buttons & Lace and talk to Charlotte. Last time I was there, I only saw casual jumpsuits, but she could probably order something for me."

Eager to stop by the boutique before going back to Brewed Haven, Rina gave Philippa a quick hug and left.

As Philippa refocused on work, her phone rang. It was Dominic.

Smiling she answered, "Hey, stranger."

"Stranger? You just saw me yesterday."

"Did I? The kiss in the walk-in was so quick, I thought I imagined it."

He chuckled, and the sound curled through her,

fading softly like whispers of smoke. "Well, I guess you should come see me for a refresher."

"Are you standing in my walk-in right now?"

"No, but I'm at the cottage. We had to delay filming at the bee farm. Apparently, the bees weren't having a good day, so we're testing a mac and cheese recipe for the show. We're using the fresh cheese we picked up from the dairy. Can you take a break and come give us an opinion?"

"Does giving an opinion come with a kiss for dessert?"

"I can probably come up with something."

"I'm on my way."

In the car, her conversation with Rina about being with a celebrity drifted into her thoughts along with Rina giving Scott "reminders."

Philippa chuckled. No wonder Scott was racking up frequent flyer miles coming back to Maryland so often. But if all went as Scott and Rina had planned, he would move to Bolan and the two of them would be together.

But with her and Dominic the situation was different. He was committed to his show and his restaurants.

If it was this difficult for Dominic to fit an afternoon into his schedule, a long-distance relationship would be even harder. *Sounds like what Chef LeBlanc had mentioned all over again…*

Whoa. Hold on. Philippa pulled herself out of the downward spiral the thought started to take her. It wasn't the same. They were established in their careers now and didn't have to work so hard to prove themselves. With a few adjustments and coordinating, they could at least try to make it work. But she was getting way too ahead of herself. What had she told Dominic? They were taking it one day at a time and that meant not projecting into the future. At least, not yet.

At the entrance to the cottage, security opened the barrier and waved her in. The vans that the crew were using to get around town weren't taking up space behind Dominic's rental like they had been lately. Did that mean there were fewer people around today?

Philippa parked, then went inside the back door, which was unlocked. Inside the entryway, she followed the smell of delicious food wafting in the air to the kitchen.

Now that the white-topped granite island, a full complement of high-end appliances, and wood cabinets were installed, the brightly lit space was an intimate and welcoming atmosphere.

In the living room area, rolled-up black cables, camera equipment, and folded-up director's chairs sat near the side walls.

Teale and Dominic stood at the island, dressed

in their work clothes. On top of the granite surface, steam rose from four square casserole dishes of mac and cheese, baked to a perfect golden brown. Bottles of water were also on the island.

Teale waved. "Hi, Philippa."

"Hello." Philippa stood next to Dominic.

He glanced over at her and smiled. "Thanks for agreeing to give us another opinion."

"Mac and cheese. I wouldn't miss it. So, are you not featuring the mac and cheese bites we're serving during cocktail hour at the party?"

"We're featuring both," Dominic replied. "The bites and a variation of traditional baked mac and cheese. We're trying to decide on the variation."

"What have you narrowed it down to so far?"

Teale pointed to the dishes as Dominic spooned a modest amount from the first one on three small plates. "We have traditional mac and cheese as the control. The variation we choose has to stack up to it as far as texture, mouthfeel and flavor. The first variation is sun-dried tomato and truffle oil. The second is seafood. We used a mixture of lobster and crab."

Philippa accepted the plate and a fork from Dominic. They all took bites. The traditional dish with a blending of different cheeses hit high marks on every level.

After sips of water, they moved on to the second. After more sips of water, they tasted the third.

"What do you think?" Teale asked.

Philippa set her fork on her plate. "Well, the tartness of the sun-dried tomatoes and the earthy flavor of truffle oil really blends well together. With the seafood variation, I'm tasting a Creole-type seasoning that's balancing out the sweetness of the lobster and crab. I like that, too."

Dominic studied her as he took a sip of bottled water. He set it down and placed the cap on it. "What's your pick?"

Her pick? The two of them spending the afternoon alone someplace where kisses were the priority, along with sharing a plate of mac and cheese while tucked under the bed covers. And maybe a nap to help erase the shadows from under his eyes. But unfortunately, those options weren't on the menu.

She pointed to the seafood variation. "That one. The Creole seasoning gives it just the right amount of kick."

Teale smiled. "I like that one, too." Her phone rang on the counter, and she checked the screen. "I need to take this." She walked into the living room space.

Unable to resist temptation, Philippa put a little more of the traditional mac and cheese on her plate. "Change is nice, but I don't think anything can beat a really good basic mac and cheese."

She ate a bite of the pasta dish. As she licked cheese sauce from her lower lip, she glanced up and saw Dominic staring at her mouth.

He cleared his throat. "Yeah, I agree. There's nothing like an original."

The huskiness in his tone raised daring, desire, and her curiosity. Clearly Rina's reminders had snagged Scott's attention when it came to making time for enjoyment as a couple. Did the busy Chef Extraordinaire need the same kind of nudge? It wouldn't hurt to try. And it could be fun.

"What type of cheese is in this? I can't quite place it. Wait don't tell me." Philippa took another bite of food. She released a quiet moan, making a show of drawing the fork slowly from her mouth. "Oh, I got it. Cheddar, Swiss and Parmesan...and Gouda. Definitely, Gouda."

As Dominic looked at her, he swallowed hard. "Yeah, definitely Gouda. You got that right."

He lifted his bottled water partway to his mouth before realizing the cap was still on.

She barely repressed a smile.

As he took a sip of water, she leaned in and whispered to him, "You know, this mac and cheese may be the best thing I've ever had. Well, maybe not the best. There is something that's much, much better and I really enjoyed it."

Dominic put the cap back on the water and set it down. "There is?"

She took him in from head to booted feet and back up again. "Oh definitely." As she met his gaze, she pictured what she wanted him to see. Desire enveloping her from the inside out.

The look in Dominic's eyes made her heart speed up. He glanced around to Teale.

Her back was to them as she chatted on the phone.

He moved closer and flattened his palm low on Philippa's back. "I think we should go to the main room down the hall. We're using it for storage." He leaned near her cheek, and his faintly whiskered one grazed over hers. "I've got some new cookware you should see. And I should probably deliver on the promise of dessert."

Dominic moved his hand a bit lower, and a rush of desire made her shiver. As much as she wanted to take him up on his offer right then, she wasn't ready to concede in the flirting game yet. She was holding out for a bigger payoff.

Philippa brushed her lips lightly over his ear as she whispered to him, "I'd love to check out your impressive cookware and sample dessert, but I have to go." She stepped out of reach with a smile on her face.

"Wait. You're leaving?"

"Yes. Priorities. You know how it is."

Dominic's incredulous expression pulled a laugh out of her.

The look on his face shifted to one of understanding, and a sinful smile curled up his lips. "Priorities. That's a good one. You do know what they say about payback, don't you?"

"You mean like turnabout is fair play?"

Dominic took a step toward her. "Exactly."

"I'm still a little confused by what you mean. If you care to explain it to me. I'll be home around eight."

His steady gaze stayed on her as she backed out of the kitchen.

As she reached her car, a text from him pinged on her phone.

You're in trouble.

Internally, she happy danced as she texted back.

I'm counting on it.

See you at eight.

The hours crawled by at a snail's pace until she finally left Pasture Lane. She had enough time to get ready for Dominic. What should she wear? Something flirty or downright sexy?

Eight o'clock at her place, she checked her hair and makeup in the mirror hanging by the entryway. Behind her, the low light from a corner lamp in the living room added a rosy glow to the beige furniture with an assortment of throw pillows with a pink, blue and green design.

She adjusted the shoulder strap of her coral-pink sundress. Flirty—that was the right choice, wasn't it?

Five after eight came and went, and her heart practically sank to her bare feet. Had something come up and he couldn't get away?

The sound of tires crunching on gravel made her heart leap and she peeked out the living room window.

Dominic got out of a black SUV, and as he walked up the steps, the car pulled out of the driveway.

She opened the door before he had a chance to ring the bell.

He was still dressed in his uniform.

He walked in and she backed up. From the look in his eyes as he shut and locked the door behind him, she really was in trouble. The good kind.

"Oh…" Desire and anticipation took away her ability to form sentences.

A faint trace of humor broke through the desire in Dominic's eyes. "'Oh'? After the torture you put me through, is that all you have to say to me?"

"Sorry…not sorry." Laughing, Philippa made a run for it, and he chased her down the adjoining hallway. Sure, she deserved payback for teasing him, but why make it easy, for him?

She reached her bedroom near the end of the hall, and Dominic was on her heels. But as she backed farther inside the room lit up softly by a bedside lamp, he paused.

Instead of coming for her, he started unbuttoning his gray chef's jacket, holding her gaze as he took his time. After he dropped the jacket, he moved on to his black pull-on shirt.

Riveted by the ripple of muscles in his abs, chest and arms, she dropped down on the bed.

As his shirt joined his jacket on the floor, he moved on to unfasten his boots. A self-assured smile ghosted over his mouth as she continued to watch him.

When the rest of his clothing finally joined the pile on the floor, he approached the bed. In between heated kisses, he removed hers.

Dominic nudged her back and stretched out beside her on the bed.

Philippa's breathing shallowed as the evidence of his desire pressed to her thigh. Her own need made her tremble as his slow caresses and the brush of his lips moved down her throat and whispered over the tips of her breasts...her belly...and between her thighs.

She arched up as he teased, pleased, and took his time. Breathy moans poured out of her as Dominic kept her hovering on the precipice. It wasn't enough. She ached for her climax that was just out of reach.

Impatience…her greatest weakness next to him. He knew her too well.

Chapter Fifteen

Philippa sat in the canvas director's chair in the portable trailer, remaining as still as possible as the auburn-haired makeup artist lined her lips.

What had she been thinking when she'd agreed to tape an episode of Dominic's show with him? Clearly, she hadn't been thinking. Probably because she'd been so into him. Holding back the smile that wanted to take over her mouth, Philippa let her mind wander through all that had taken place since the day of the mac and cheese tasting.

He'd started coming to her house at night whenever he could get away after a day of filming. But that wasn't a simple task. At the cottage, Dominic would slip into the back seat of the SUV driven by one of the private security specialists he'd brought in from LA. On their way to the hotel up the road where the security team was staying, they'd drop Dominic off at her place.

Once he arrived, they usually cooked a meal together, watched movies, talked…and made love. But he never stayed until morning.

Long before sunrise, the routine was repeated in reverse as the security specialist now going to the cottage for his guard duty shift would pick Dominic up.

The paparazzi or local journalists weren't hounding him yet, but as they ramped up for the event in two weeks and the stars of *Shadow Valley*, including Chloe Daniels, arrived in Bolan, more of them would be in town. Adhering to the current security plan would help keep him and Philippa off their radar for now.

"Okay, you're all set." The makeup artist removed the protective paper collar from around Philippa's neck.

The middle-aged woman had skillfully filled in Philippa's brows, enhanced her cheekbones and given her natural-looking lush lips.

"Thank you." Philippa rose from the chair, carrying a copy of the one-page script.

Walking out the wide trailer onto the grassy field overlooking the strawberry patch at Crossroads, a pick-your-own-fruit-and-vegetables farm near Bolan, she struggled to remember what to do next. The hoard of butterflies turning somersaults in her belly kept distracting her.

The film crew and other members of Dominic's team, including Eve, bustled in and out of the other three trailers and extended vans, also parked in the field, almost in a row.

Chloe was supposed to be there, too, but Philippa hadn't seen her since she'd arrived close to an hour ago. Or Dominic.

Farther down on the right, John, the blond production assistant, emerged from in between a trailer and a van. The slender, serious-looking guy was dressed in tennis shoes, jeans and a black *Dinner with Dominic* T-shirt with CREW printed on the back.

As he hurried over to her, he talked to someone on his headset as he looked at the screen of the computer tablet he carried. "Yes, the talent is ready. I'm bringing them to you now." John looked up and his face morphed into a smile. "Chef Gayle, you look great. Follow me."

Philippa fast-walked with him. Maybe she should have worn her tennis shoes instead of her boots with her chef's uniform. "How far do we have to walk to get to the set?"

"Oh, no, you don't have to walk. I'm zipping you over there in a golf cart, and I'll bring you back here afterward so the driver can take you home."

The two-hour journey there by private car had been nice, and the driver had been courteous. But it had also been lonely.

When Dominic and his director had talked her into this, she'd envisioned her and Dominic riding to the farm together, taking in the sights along the way. Of course, that didn't make sense. Coming to Crossroads Farms wasn't a romantic road trip.

As promised, John took her where today's set was located.

The area with empty stalls covered by green-and-white-striped awnings was where the farmers' market took place on the weekends. An intimate outdoor restaurant, reserved tables only, was also opened for lunch and dinner right next to it during that time. Customers enjoyed a limited menu featuring produce they picked, prepared tableside.

She and Rina had tried it out once and loved it, but the long drive there and back had been a bit much.

A tall bistro-style table sat in the middle of a grassy space amid the stalls. Cameras, lighting and other filming equipment along with a director's chair were positioned a few yards away from it.

John walked her to a spot off to the side. He left for a moment and returned with a canvas chair. "Have a seat. Someone will mic you up soon. I'll be nearby. Let me know if you need anything."

"Thank you."

Crew members bustled around the area. They

moved equipment. Checked the lighting as well as the distances, from different angles, from the camera to the table.

Where was Dominic? Would he spend a few minutes with her before the filming started? It would help to see his face right now. As time passed without seeing him, her disappointment and anxiety started to increase.

"Hi, Philippa." Chloe waved.

As she strolled toward Philippa, a light breeze lifted her wavy black hair from her shoulders, and the skirt of her casual purple dress flowed around her thighs. She made traversing across the grass in heels appear effortless.

When she reached Philippa, she gave her a big hug. "Uh-oh. I know that look. It's called nervous."

Philippa returned the embrace, relieved to see a familiar face. "I can't believe I got talked into this."

As John appeared with a chair for Chloe, another young, dark-haired guy with kind hazel eyes came over with two lavalier microphones.

He turned to Philippa. "This needs to be inside your jacket so it won't show on camera. Is it alright if I attached it?"

"That's fine." She opened the top buttons of her jacket and he clipped it on the inside, near the top of her chest.

He handed her a black box the size of a deck of

cards. "This is the receiver. I'll let you tuck this into a pocket. That side one on your pants leg looks good."

Philippa stuck it in her pocket and buttoned it closed.

Chloe taped on her own mic and tucked the receiver into a discreet side pocket in the skirt of her dress.

After thanking John and the sound guy, she settled into the chair next to Philippa. "You're going to be just fine."

"I don't feel fine. I woke up feeling nauseous. I don't know how to act."

"That's the best part. You don't have to. From what I saw when I glanced at the script, it calls for you and Dominic to have an ordinary chef-to-chef conversation about food, just like you would if the crew and cameras weren't around."

"Let me guess. I'm supposed to pretend that they're not there."

"Yeah, that's the expectation." Chloe chuckled but empathy reflected in her brown eyes. "I know it's intimidating to have cameras in your face. But Dominic and I are experienced at doing this. Just follow our lead, and we'll get you through it."

A brunette, dressed like John, drove Dominic on set in a golf cart. After thanking the woman, he got out and strode toward Philippa and Chloe. He was more than impressive looking in a navy chef's jacket rolled up to his forearms, paired with black pants and boots.

As he approached the table, his gaze met Philippa's and he smiled.

Her heart kicked in a few extra beats. He looked so wonderful. She could sit there and stare at him forever.

"Hi, ladies. It's good to see you." Dominic gave Philippa an impersonal hug. He smelled just as wonderful as he looked. He turned and hugged Chloe. "Thanks for doing this on such short notice."

Chloe smoothed a curl from her forehead and smiled. "Happy to help. And you promised me food. How could I resist?"

Brianne, the show's dark haired assistant director, came over to them. After greeting everyone, she walked them through the scene. "Dominic, we'll do the intro for this clip later. Chloe, we want your genuine reaction to what you're tasting, so don't hold back." She looked to Philippa. "This is just a natural conversation between you, Dominic and Chloe about the menu. Do what you'd normally do in a food-tasting situation. Just pretend the rest of us aren't here."

Chloe arched a brow at Philippa with a friendly I-told-you-so look on her face.

It couldn't be that simple. Could it?

In a flurry of activity, the crew handled camera adjustments as the makeup artist and stylist made last-minute touch-ups to Dominic, Philippa and Chloe's hair and makeup.

Eve brought two picture-perfect salads to the table. Sliced orange-and-blush peaches added bright pops of color to the summer slaw, and lemon wedges along with lemony dressing gave the grilled romaine a fresh appeal.

Once the salads were in place, Eve and the stylist cleared the set.

As Dominic and Philippa took their places around the high table, he gave her hand a light squeeze, and she glanced at him.

His wink combined with a slight, sexy smile created chaos with her heart rate, already on overload from nerves.

Not helping... The mics hanging above them and the one clipped near her chest caused her to hold back in saying it. She stared at Dominic, hoping he'd get the hint.

His smile broadened, and from the look of satisfaction on his face, he knew what type of an affect he had on her.

Philippa's nerves lessened a bit as she released a quiet chuckle and slowly shook her head at him.

"Alright." Brianne peered at a monitor. "Looks good. Quiet everyone. Action."

As if he'd flipped a switch, Dominic kicked off the conversational scene. "Chef Gayle and I have narrowed the salad choices down to these two. A summer slaw with charred peppers and peaches with a miso dressing. And grilled romaine topped with applewood-smoked bacon, fresh Parmesan, a dusting of crushed sourdough croutons and drizzled with a creamy lemon dressing." He turned to Philippa. "So, which one do you think is best?"

Upbeat banter... That was something the script mentioned. She looked up from the salad at Dominic. But they didn't banter. They traded opinions and took sides.

"I like the slaw, but I'm leaning toward the grilled romaine. The combination of the char on the lettuce, the smokiness of the bacon and the zesty flavor of the lemon reminds me of summer grilling season. It's simple, but it also has upscale flair. It's almost a reflection of the event."

Dominic's eyes lit up with approval. "I definitely see and taste what you're saying, but I also think this summer slaw fits in with the event in the same way. It's a complex mix of flavors with the cabbage, peppers and peaches. But the peaches, along with the fresh cilantro, basil and mint, give it a fresh summer appeal, which gives the salad its name."

"But a name isn't what makes a recipe." Philippa smiled. "It's all about taste."

"True." He chuckled good-naturedly. "I think we're going to need help with this decision, which is why I gave Chloe Daniels a call."

"Hey, you two." Chloe waved as she approached them.

Hugs were exchanged, and then Dominic spelled out their dilemma.

Just like Chloe promised, she and Dominic took the lead, making it easier for Philippa to forget about the cameras and follow them through the conversation.

After Chloe tasted the salads, she set down her fork. "Wow. This is so hard. I love the fresh peaches in the slaw, but who can say no to bacon with the grilled romaine?" Her expression grew thoughtful. "Why can't we have both of them?"

That wasn't a bad idea. Philippa chimed in, "A sampling of both—I like it."

Dominic stroked his chin with a contemplative expression. Then he smiled. "I can get on board with that."

"Yay," Chloe cheered. "I can't wait to enjoy them at the party."

A beat or two later, Brianne yelled out. "Cut. Good job, guys."

Chloe looked Philippa up and down. "You go, girl. Handling yourself like a pro."

A smile took over Philippa's mouth as she exchanged a high five with her. "You two made it easy."

Dominic lightly placed his hand on Philippa's waist. "She's right. You were great. I knew you would be."

She leaned into him, and as his gaze dropped to

her mouth, the temptation to kiss him almost overwhelmed her. "Thanks."

"I like all of this. And I want more." Chloe made a gesture encompassing them and the salads. "Tristan and I are going out for bar food at the Montecito. It's karaoke night. We don't sing. We sit in a corner and watch. Do you want to come with? It's usually calm—hardly anyone asks for a picture or an autograph."

Dominic looked to Philippa. "We'll be done here in a couple of hours. I'm in if you are."

"But don't you have a conference call with your sister tonight?" He'd mentioned it yesterday.

"I'll squeeze in a short one with her beforehand."

A night out with Dominic—like a date? No, it wouldn't be like a real date because they wouldn't be able to act like a couple. "Sure, I can make it."

"Sounds like a plan." Enthusiasm lit up his eyes. "What time are we meeting up?"

Hours later, Philippa tucked her keys into her shoulder bag and walked up the steps to the porch of the Montecito Steakhouse alone.

She entered the semifull corridor between the bar and the dining area of the dark-wood-and-brick restaurant and veered left to the bar.

The place was fairly busy for a Thursday night. Most of the stools at the bar up-front were occupied with people watching the flat screens featuring sports channels. Empty tables dotted the semicrowded main floor, and a few people played pool and darts at the side of the room.

After changing four times, she'd chosen the right outfit. Thank goodness. Because of her job, she spent most of her days, buttoned up in a chef's jacket wearing a pair of clogs. Slipping into her strappy stilettos, form-fitting jeans, and pink-and-blue-patterned boho sleeveless blouse was a nice change, along with ditching the headband she wore in the kitchen. And she didn't have to worry about staying out too late. Tomorrow, she had the morning and most of the afternoon off.

She spotted Chloe waving her over to a corner booth on the other side of the room. Tristan sat beside her. Chloe still wore the same dress from the taping at the farm. Tristan was also casual in a tan shirt and jeans.

Over the past few years, Philippa had socialized with Tristan at staff gatherings and at Rina's house. She'd also hung out with Chloe numerous times in the past year, including helping to organize Chloe's bridal shower, but Philippa had never gone on a couples' outing with them.

It was a little strange. And joining them on her own made her feel a tad awkward.

"Hi... Hey." Chloe and Tristan greeted Philippa at the same time.

She gave them both a smile and a general wave before she took her bag off her shoulder and sat down.

Tucked in the middle of the curved seat next to Tristan, Chloe patted the space next to her, prompting Philippa to slide closer.

As Tristan took a pull from his bottle of beer, he glanced toward the room, then back to Philippa. "I thought Dominic was coming?"

"His meeting with his sister ran longer than anticipated, but he's on his way. He said we should start without him." And coming in separate cars helped protect their undercover relationship.

"I'll put in a food order at the bar," Tristan said. "It's faster than waiting for a server." He looked to Philippa. "Cajun wings, ribs and loaded nachos okay?"

"Sounds good to me."

After finding out what Philippa wanted to drink and if Chloe wanted another glass of red wine, he headed for the bar.

Chloe sat back in the booth. "You did a really good job today with the segment. I honestly don't know what you were worried about."

"Thank you. It means a lot to hear you say that. I was so afraid of messing up."

"That was never going to happen. You held your own. Dominic wouldn't have asked you if he didn't think you could. He's the star of a hit show. It doesn't matter that you're his girlfriend, he can't afford to be charitable about who he puts in front of the camera."

"Girlfriend? No. Dominic and I are old acquaintances and colleagues."

"You do realize I can see right through Publicist 101–speak. And I felt the sparks between you two this afternoon, so I'm not buying it."

"That obvious, huh?"

"Just a tad." Chloe laughed, but then her expression sobered. "But I get why you're not making things public. It can get rough. Coming back to Bolan is a relief for me. The novelty of me being with Tristan died down after the wedding. And a lot of the people around here don't care that I was in a movie. I'm just Chloe Tillbridge walking down the street. But that could change once *Shadow Valley* releases next week."

It may have been rough, but Chloe and Tristan gave off strong power-couple energy when they were together. "How do you and Tristan handle the attention so well?"

"One moment at a time." Chloe looked toward Tristan at the bar and smiled softly. "And he understands that what we share as a couple is fact. Anything that's put out for public consumption about us, especially in the media, is highly speculative." She glanced past Philippa and pointed. "He's here."

Philippa joined Chloe in waving down Dominic. He wove through the tables and the crowd, making it to the corner booth without anyone stopping him, and sat next to Philippa.

He'd changed into dark jeans and a black pullover. Outfit-wise they were a perfect match on their first couples' date.

"Sorry I'm so late." His gaze met Philippa's before encompassing Chloe. "Next round's on me. Where's Tristan?"

"Waiting for drinks at the bar. I should go help him. Do you know what you want?" Chloe asked Dominic as she slid out the other side of the booth.

"Beer's fine."

Once Chloe left, Philippa looked to Dominic. A small frown tugged down his mouth as he stared at his hand on the table. "Did your call with Bailey go okay?"

He gave her a lopsided smile. "It could have gone better."

"What happened?"

Dominic scratched over his brow. "I lost a big investor in the Atlanta restaurant."

"Oh, no, I'm sorry. Why are they pulling out?"

"Not sure." He released a harsh breath. "They just said the project wasn't a right fit for them anymore."

Philippa angled herself toward him. "Will this delay opening the restaurant?"

"Not if we can find another investor. I have to go back to LA day after tomorrow for a few meetings."

"How long will you be gone?"

"A few days, maybe. But I'll be back in time for the party. I'm sorry that I'm leaving at a critical time and dropping it all on you."

"You're not dropping anything on me. The menu's finalized. The food is ordered. Coordination for the setup and the help we need is on track. There isn't much left to do. But what about your show?"

"We might be able to squeeze in one more episode at the cottage after the screening party. We'll have to tape the rest of them at the set kitchen in LA. As far as the rest of the farm segments, the crew will film some general footage of the places I didn't get to visit, and we'll add my voice-over to them."

The dejected look on his face made her heart go out to him.

He'd really been looking forward to his upcoming visits to the bee farm and the local farm vineyard and winery. They were using honey from the bee farm in one of the sauces and serving wine from the vineyard at the party. He'd planned to highlight both on his show.

Under the table, Philippa laid her hand on his thigh in a comforting gesture. "Anything I can do to help?"

He laid his hand on hers. "No, but I have to tell you something." He opened his mouth to say more.

Tristan and Chloe returned with drinks, and a server followed with their food.

"We're back." Chloe set a bottle of beer in front of Dominic.

The server put down the food, plates and utensils as Chloe and Tristan slid into the booth.

Dominic gave Philippa's hand a brief squeeze before letting go. He leaned closer and spoke in a low voice for only her to hear. "Let's enjoy being out tonight. We'll talk later."

They all dug into the food.

Chloe talked about the upcoming, red-carpet premier of the movie in LA the following week. Tristan would attend with her.

"And review time is always interesting." Chloe shook her head. "I can't bring myself to read them when they go up."

"You were fantastic in *Shadow Valley.*" Tristan kissed her cheek. "That's all you need to know."

Loud hoots of laughter traveled across the bar from a group headed toward seats near the pool table. A willowy tanned, dark-haired woman in a short flowy white dress and brown cowboy boots seemed to be the ringleader of the group.

Chloe stared that direction. "She looks familiar."

Something about her was familiar to Philippa, too. "Who is she?"

Dominic put down his beer. "Destiny Mitchell."

Scowling, he stood. "I'll be right back." He stalked off toward the group.

"Wait. Isn't she his ex?" Chloe asked.

Tristan paused in the middle of eating nachos.

"Yes, that's her." Unease built inside of Philippa as Destiny threw her arms around Dominic.

"Well." Chloe's gaze narrowed. "She's definitely not invited to our table."

Chapter Sixteen

Dominic reined in frustration as he deftly took Destiny's arms from around his neck and guided her to a less crowded area near the pool table. "What are you doing here?"

Destiny gave him a puzzled look. "Didn't your sister pass along that I wanted to talk to you?"

"She said you were calling me." And he'd told Bailey to tell Destiny *not* to call him. They had nothing to talk about.

Recently, the producers of *Best Chef Wins* had pushed back about featuring him and Destiny as a couple on the reunion show. She was all in. His answer was still a hard pass.

"New York is just a few hours away, and I wanted

to have a conversation with you face-to-face. Come sit with us." She tilted her head to the side, a practiced, coy gesture aimed at breaking down resistance and getting what she wanted.

He'd quickly become immune to that during their few months together. Right around the time he'd found out her so-called friends were the ones feeding info about him and Destiny to the media. And that she knew about it. He also began to suspect her cookbook deal was nonexistent. She kept changing her story about whether she had a contract. All of that had led him to distance himself from her.

"I don't know if you're here on your own or if someone convinced you it was a good idea. Either way, you're wasting your time. I'm not doing the reunion if rekindling a fake relationship with you is part of it."

"Des and Dom." A woman hurried over to them. "I told my husband it was the two of you." She looked to Dominic. "I love your show and your cookbook. Can I get a picture with the two of you?"

"Sure." Destiny beamed.

One of Destiny's friends jumped up to take the photo.

The woman was so excited. He couldn't say no to a fan.

Making sure the woman was between him and Destiny, he conjured up a smile as the picture was taken.

"Thank you," the woman said. "My girlfriends back home in Colorado are going to be so jealous." She hurried back to her table.

Destiny turned to Dominic with a high-and-mighty expression. "Pleasing the fans. That's what the reunion show is about. That's why I've signed on to do it. You holding out is just selfish." She stalked back to her friends.

Selfish? He respected and appreciated his fans. He wasn't holding out because he was selfish. He was holding out because he didn't want to perpetuate lies about his personal life. Especially now that he and Philippa were back together.

Dominic glanced back at the corner booth. Chloe sat alone. He spotted Tristan near the pool tables, talking to Bethany and her boyfriend, Adam, who was a groom at the stable.

Did Philippa leave? Dominic swore under his breath as he wove through the crowd. He should have told Philippa about the reunion show and Destiny. He'd almost mentioned it when he sat down earlier in the booth and he and Philippa were alone. But then Chloe and Tristan and the food had showed up.

At the booth, her purse was gone. His heart dropped. "Where did Philippa go?"

Chloe glanced up at him as she ate a loaded chip. She held up her finger, telling him to wait as she chewed. Finally she finished. "Ladies' room. And that's all I know."

Dominic exhaled in relief as he dropped down on the padded seat. "Can you at least tell me if she's upset?"

Chloe said nothing, but the look she gave him said everything.

He should know the answer to that question. "Destiny being here is not what it looks like."

"So I should hold off on digging up my vintage Des & Dom T-shirt?"

"Definitely?" Did she really have one?

Chloe picked up a pile of nachos with a fork and put it on her plate. "Balancing reality and perception are what we have to do. I get it. But people outside our industry don't always see it that way. I almost lost Tristan because I wasn't viewing my situation from his perspective."

"What did you do to fix it?"

"I set boundaries with other people. And I made sure he was clear on where we stood as a couple. He knows I have obligations, but he also understands that he's an important part of my life. The last thing a relationship needs is doubt." Her gaze shifted from him to across the room. "She's coming back." Chloe's gaze came back to him. "Whatever you need to say to straighten things out with her, don't wait. Tell her now. You might not get another chance."

"I know." He'd already made the mistake of not telling her earlier about the situation with Destiny and the reunion. He wouldn't do that again.

Tristan returned and slid back into the booth next to Chloe. He looked between her and Dominic. "So…is everything okay?"

Chloe held a chip near Tristan's mouth. "It will be when you order more appetizers."

Tristan grinned. "Already on it. Cheese fries and jalapeño poppers are on the way." He ate the chip and Chloe kissed him.

Stay ahead of the curve and take nothing for granted. Tristan had the right game plan. Envy and disappointment in himself pinged solidly in Dominic. He had to get his act together if he didn't want to lose Philippa.

She arrived at the table, and he stood to let her in the booth.

As she scooted next to Chloe, she plunked her purse down next to him, as if putting a barrier between them.

Ignoring him, she looked toward the karaoke DJ set up off to the side.

Just as he leaned in to speak to her, music blasted through the speakers and the crowd grew livelier.

A small group of women stood near the area huddled around a song menu. Laughing, they all pointed to each other as if trying to determine who should go first.

A moment later one of them stood in front of the monitor with a mic.

Strains of a ballad sung by Adele floated through the bar. The self-conscious woman quietly sang the opening line slightly off key. But as her friends cheered her on, she settled into the lyrics and grew more confident.

Philippa swayed in her seat to the music.

Was it corny to get up and dance to karaoke? No one in the bar was, but did it matter? Especially if he could erase any doubts in Philippa's mind about his commitment to their relationship?

Dominic stood and held his hand out to Philippa. "Dance with me?"

Her eyes popped wide as she swallowed a bite of nachos. "To this? Now?"

"Yes. Now. And the song doesn't matter. I want to dance…with you."

Smiling, Chloe nudged her. "Go on."

Philippa took his hand and got up. He led her to a clear spot a few feet from the karaoke equipment, then pulled her close, holding her by the waist.

She hesitated a beat before resting her hands on his chest. Hints of confusion and concern were in her gaze as she glanced around the bar. "Maybe we shouldn't do this. People are staring."

"I don't care. I'm with you, not Destiny. And I want everyone here and outside this place to know we're together. I don't want to pretend we're not anymore." Maybe it wasn't the ideal way to break the news of their relationship, but he was tired of pretending.

Nodding in agreement, Philippa relaxed in his arms.

As he brought her closer and laid his forehead to hers, Philippa slid her hands up and around his neck and closed her eyes.

The ballad about true love floated over them, and soon they swayed slowly, nearly cheek to cheek.

I could hold you for a million years to make you feel my love…

The lyrics of the song reflected everything he wanted her to know and hoped their relationship could be.

During a break in the song where the lyrics paused, the music swelled and so did a strange feeling in his chest.

"I love you." Stunned that the declaration slipped out of him, he missed a step.

As she looked up at him, surprise and a soft, happy smile lit up Philippa's face. "I love you, too."

Relief came over him, and he kissed her softly, fighting the urge to deepen the kiss as her lips curved into a smile against his.

"Hey, you two," Chloe stage-whispered as she danced nearby with Tristan. "Cut that out, or go make out in the car already."

Philippa glanced at Chloe and laughed, a pure sound, filled with joy.

As her eyes met his, a mix of emotions hit him all at once. Desire, love, the need to take care of her and keep her safe—they intertwined inside of him along with a hint of fear.

He couldn't mess this up. No matter what, he'd make sure she was happy. He'd show her in every way he could just how much she mattered to him. How much he needed her. Starting when they got to her place later on. Dominic kissed her again. But until then, he'd have to be content with a dance.

That night, at Philippa's house, they went inside and he locked the door.

"Tonight was fun." Philippa leaned over to slip off her sandals.

"It was."

She stood up straight, and the lure of her lush lips was too much of a temptation. He gave into it and pressed his mouth to hers. The kiss took them from zero to burning passion in an instant.

In the bedroom, they undressed each other, and his world narrowed to fervent caresses and heated kisses. Gliding into Philippa, he was lost, blinded by need that he couldn't control.

Afterward, sated from passion, he held her in his arms, content and happy for the first time in…he couldn't remember. And he didn't want to give it up to travel back to LA. Or to be on a reunion show.

You holding out is just selfish...

Destiny's words played in his mind. Bailey had said pretty much the same thing when he'd wanted to pull out of the screening party.

What they called *selfish* felt like self-preservation, because lately it had started to feel as if he had nothing. But around Philippa it felt as if he had something. And whatever it was, he didn't want to lose it.

A couple of hours before sunrise, Philippa stuck a hazelnut coffee pod in the coffee maker on her black granite counter. She started the machine and the scent that always perked up her morning filled the air.

Her growling stomach had woken her up earlier. Maybe it was because of all the extra activity she'd put in with Dominic last night. Unable to go back to sleep, she'd gotten up without waking him. He'd looked so peaceful in her bed. She'd lingered, taking in the sight of him.

And that's when the idea had come to her. Breakfast.

They hadn't shared a morning meal at her house yet. And they had time to enjoy it before his security showed up to take him back to Tillbridge.

As she sipped coffee, she sorted through a mental list of current ingredients in her kitchen and settled on what to make.

Reaching into the hammered-copper bread box,

she took out the loaf of brioche. Then she grabbed a bowl from under the counter and took a whisk from the drawer. From memory, she mixed milk, eggs, vanilla, sugar and spices in a bowl. In no time, slices of brioche sizzled in a skillet with butter and syrup warmed in a pan on the stove.

Dominic walked into the kitchen, sniffing the air. "French toast?"

"Yes. And you're just in time."

As she slid the golden, toasted slices from the nonstick skillet onto a couple of plates, Dominic hugged her from behind and kissed the side of her neck. "Thank you."

"You're welcome."

A short time later, they sat on the high-backed stools next to the tall kitchen counter and communed over their food in companionable silence.

Cinnamon, nutmeg, allspice and buttery sweetness flowed over her taste buds.

Dominic swirled the last bit of his French toast around his plate, gathering up leftover syrup. "I haven't tasted French toast like this in a while." He finished the bite. "Allspice, huh? How much?"

"Just a dash."

He chuckled. "Got it. So this is one of those recipes that lives in your head, no measurements needed."

"Yeah. I've been making it since I arrived at Tillbridge."

He sat back on the high-backed stool. "How did you end up at Tillbridge?"

During their past conversations, they hadn't gotten to that topic.

"Well." She pulled the pieces of the story together in her mind. "I'd decided to leave DC and move to Philadelphia. I was driving there. I didn't have to be to work for two weeks. I already had a place to live, so I was taking my time. Someone had mentioned that the best chili they'd ever tasted had come from this food van at a horse stable. I was intrigued."

"So, like all foodies lured by the claim of the best, you had to check it out."

Philippa chuckled. "Yeah, I did. And I met the van's cook, Hollis Prescott, or Hollie as everyone called him. He was seventy years old with the energy of someone half his age. He'd worked for Tillbridge as a groom for years, and he was also known for his food. He used to cook meals for the staff on a grill, set up near the parking lot.

Five years before I met him, a horse had crushed his foot. It became too difficult for him to do his job and he had to retire. But he missed being around everyone, and they missed his food, so he started going to the stable during the week to cook for them. He purchased the van so he wouldn't have to miss a day because of cold or bad weather. Eventually, it turned into a bona fide business."

Dominic picked up their plates. "So many great places start out like that. Someone cooking for the love of it and it turning into something more."

In her mind, she could see Hollie's smile light up his brown face through his white beard. "He really did cook with love and didn't mind sharing it. When I told him why I'd come to his food van, he invited me to come back the next day to see how he made his famous chili. I did, and ended up helping serve it to his customers."

"Smart man. He put you to work." Dominic rinsed the plates in the sink and put them in the dishwasher.

"I didn't mind. I loved talking to him. He'd led a fascinating life. He'd grown up in Texas. Joined the navy at eighteen. Got out and joined the merchant marines. He'd married twice. Lost both wives and didn't have any children. After he lost his second wife, the love of his life, he'd been on his way to Maine to become a deckhand on a lobster boat. A wrong turn had put him at Tillbridge, and he never left."

Dominic came back to the stool and sat down. "Sounds like what happened was meant to be."

He took hold of her hand on the counter and intertwined their fingers. It was a natural gesture that happened with ease, as if they'd sat there hundreds of times and he'd done that very thing.

Philippa continued the story. "I didn't want to

leave, either, after helping him for two more days. I came by the van the third day to say goodbye to Hollie, but it was closed. I found out he'd had a heart attack. I went to see him and decided to stay the night. He was so upbeat and optimistic about his surgery. I just knew he'd make it."

As if sensing what was coming next, Dominic held her hand a bit tighter.

"I was devastated. I'd envisioned coming back to see him, helping him in the van and enjoying one of our long talks." Remembered sadness tightened Philippa's throat.

"I kept thinking about our talks as I was driving to Philadelphia and halfway there, I turned back.

"The Tillbridges were in charge of Hollie's affairs. I wanted to buy the van from them and take over where Hollie had left off. They said they couldn't sell it to me, but they could give it to me. Before the surgery, Hollie had updated his will and he'd left it to me. He believed I'd come back. Less than year later, I was opening Pasture Lane."

Pride and respect for her bloomed inside of him. "I'm not surprised you were successful." Her kissed her hand. "How did the restaurant happen? Did you approach the Tillbridge's with the idea?"

"I—"

The sound of a car engine filtered in, and they both looked to the front of the house.

Breakfast was over. Dominic had to leave.

Philippa smiled through her disappointment. "Your ride is here."

Chapter Seventeen

Dominic battled reluctance as he retrieved his wallet and phone from Philippa's bedroom. He sent a text to the security specialist waiting in the SUV that he was on his way out to meet them.

Waking up to be with Philippa and having breakfast together had been so relaxing. And he'd enjoyed finding out more about her career and the things she'd experienced along the way.

But the moment had ended too soon. And since he was flying to California tomorrow, they wouldn't get a chance to kick back like this for a while considering the upcoming event and their schedules.

Dominic went back down the hall and joined

her at the front door. He indulged in a long kiss with Philippa.

It would have to tide him over at least for a few hours. He and the crew were filming at the bee farm that morning.

Maybe he and Philippa could meet up for a late lunch. "What time are you going into the restaurant today?"

"Close to the start of dinner. I have a ton of housework to do." As Philippa leaned away, she caressed up and down his back. "Quinn is in charge until I get there, I'm hoping the responsibility will boost her confidence."

Dominic squashed his planned lunch invitation. "Can we meet up later tonight at the cottage? I promise to kick everyone out by eight."

"I'll come by, but I'm not staying the night. You need to get some sleep before you leave."

He was flying out of Baltimore at four in the morning by private jet, and he'd hit the ground running once he landed in LA. "True. And if you stayed, you'd wake up earlier than you needed to because of me."

"Yeah, that wouldn't be any fun." She looped her arms around his neck. "But I will miss kissing you before you leave. I like your goodbye kisses."

He squeezed her waist. "Just my goodbye kisses?"

"Well…" She gave him a teasing contemplative look. "I guess your hello kisses are decent, too. On the scale of one to ten maybe they're a four."

"A four? Oh really?" He tickled Philippa's waist and nibbled a sensitive spot on the side of her neck.

Releasing a squeal of laughter, she squirmed in his arms. "Wait…stop."

"Not until you change your score."

"Intimidating the judge—that's not fair!"

Chuckling, he doubled down on the tickling.

"Okay." Philippa laughed breathlessly. "Four and a half." She escaped from his hold.

Dominic caught her by the waist again, brought her flush against him, and captured her mouth. The feel of her soft curves changed teasing into want and the kiss quickly grew heated.

Releasing a moan of disappointment, she flattened her hands to his chest and eased out of the kiss. "Go. The bees are waiting."

Dominic took a deep breath and reined himself in. Philippa's lips, swollen from the kiss, made him want to say to hell with everything but being with her.

He let her go. "See you tonight."

In the driveway, on the way to the SUV, his phone rang.

He checked the screen then answered it. "Hey, Eve, what's up?"

"Apparently, not the bees. The psychic bee farmer says today's not a good day either for us to film. Or more accurately, she said, it's not a good plan for *you* to be there today. Isn't that weird? Anyway, Brianna and Matt are working on moving up filming at the vineyard to today instead. I had a question about the wine pairings we're featuring in that segment..."

His mind drifted away from what Eve was telling him, and an idea started to form. He couldn't stop a grin. "I'm taking the morning and afternoon off."

"Excuse me?"

"And everyone else can, too. I'll be at the cottage in time to tape the episode like we planned."

"That's fine with me, but Brianne..."

"She'll be fine. I'll let everyone know. See you tonight."

He ended the call, released the security specialist to return to the cottage until he called him, and then sent the team a text.

No frills or explanations, just what he told Eve. He'd never skipped out before, but it was his show, and he had a say in his schedule. The bee farmer cancelled. He could shift his afternoon conference calls to another day. It was too easy.

After he sent it, a weight lifted from his chest, and something he hadn't felt in a long time took its place. Freedom.

Dominic jogged back up the stairs to the porch. He rang the doorbell.

A short time later, Philippa opened the door. She was clearly surprised to see him. "Hey."

Dominic strode across the threshold, cupped

her face, and laid a kiss on her that left them both breathless.

"How was that for a hello kiss?" he asked.

A dreamy expression covered Philippa's face as she blinked back at him. "That was perfect. Did you come all the way back here for that?"

He stroked her face. "Yes, kind of. Need help with your housework? I have the morning and afternoon off."

That afternoon, Dominic stirred sugar into a pitcher of fresh lemonade in Philippa's kitchen.

After they'd finished the chicken sandwiches he'd made for lunch earlier, he'd been cleaning the refrigerator and discovered a half-dozen lemons starting to dry out in the back of the crisper drawer. With all he and Philippa had accomplished in and outside the house, lemonade was the perfect reward.

Working together they'd knocked out cleaning the rooms, doing a couple of loads of laundry, and clipping a few of the hedges in half the time it would have taken Philippa on her own. Now they could just relax.

He'd even gotten the rest of the story about her and Pasture Lane Restaurant. Business at the food van had become so successful, she'd started selling basic premade dinners at night to the locals. But instead of driving back home, many of the people started utilizing the few tables she'd set up or took chairs out of their truck and tailgated.

Once Zurie had decided to build the guesthouse, it was clear a restaurant needed to be a part of it. Philippa and Zurie had approached each other at the same time. They'd negotiated terms—Philippa would have full control over the development and running of the restaurant and receive a percentage of the profits on top of her salary. From its opening day, Pasture Lane had been a success.

After pouring the lemonade into two glasses with ice, he carried them to the front porch where Philippa sat on the bench seat.

A light breeze ruffled the leaves on the trees and recently trimmed flowering hedges lined near the porch.

She looked up at him, and the gleam of happiness that had been in her eyes since their hello kiss grew even brighter. "Okay. Now you're just showing off. You cleaned, cooked, did lawn work, and now you've made fresh lemonade."

"I'm not showing off. I'm spoiling you."

She accepted the glass he handed her. "I could get used to this."

He sat on the bench seat next to her. According to Philippa, the area around them had once been farmland. The time he'd spent at Tillbridge and traveling through the countryside to visit farms, he could easily imagine cows and horses as part of the landscape. And maybe a modest-sized garden off to the side.

Dominic stretched his arm behind Philippa's back and took a sip of lemonade. "I wouldn't mind doing this again. I'm really enjoying today."

She made a face. "Even the vacuuming?"

"I'm happy about being here with you. But I have to admit, the vacuuming was pretty satisfying."

"Seriously?" She gave him a baffled look. "You find housecleaning satisfying?"

"Not always." He pulled her close and kissed her temple. "But today, wasn't just about cleaning. There was so much more to it."

Philippa's expression grew even more puzzled. "I don't understand."

He searched for the words to explain. "This place reflects who you are, and every room tells a story. The throw pillows in the living room reflect your love of color. The number of serving bowls and platters in your cabinet are a dead giveaway that you want to share your love of food. And the scent of lavender and lemon balm in your bedroom," he traced his finger over her smooth cheek. "That's the place where you're the most peaceful. This isn't just a home. It's your sanctuary."

"But isn't your house a sanctuary for you, too?"

"In a way, I guess. It serves its purpose. It's where I leave and come home to at night. It's functional."

"Oh?" For a brief second, something akin to sadness passed through Philippa's face before she covered it with a smile. She laid her head on his shoulder. "Well, that's important, too. Especially if functional was what you wanted."

When he'd bought the house a few years ago, he'd designed the studio kitchen the building contractors had added on to the house for the filming of his show.

As far as the rest of the place, he'd filled out an extensive questionnaire for the interior decorator about his style preferences and intended uses for the rooms. Weeks later, he walked into a place with clean lines and a few eye-catching details.

In the private plane the next morning, when it lifted from the runway into the dark sky, a sadness that mirrored what he'd spotted in Philippa's eyes when he'd described his house to her came over him.

Years ago, a functional house, and a functional life had suited him. Now he yearned for something that he didn't know how to describe. But the one thing he did know, whatever it was. He wanted it with Philippa.

Chapter Eighteen

Dominic walked past the host stand into the dining area of Flame & Frost LA. Afternoon heat mingling underneath his gray suit and light gray dress shirt, minus the tie, quickly dissipated.

At three in the afternoon on a Monday, the lunch crowd in the space that was a combination of clean lines, dark wood and tinted glass had thinned out.

The perfect time for a meeting, at least it was in Bailey's eyes. He would have rather been in the restaurant's kitchen. Cooking was one thing that could jolt him awake after a long flight. Earlier that afternoon, he'd made the mistake of sitting down on the couch in his home office after a series of conference calls and conked right out. He'd even slept through the reminder he'd set on his phone, making him late for the meeting.

Dreaming of holding Philippa in his arms, then waking up on his couch had been a huge disappointment. He missed her.

As he walked through the dining area, servers wearing uniforms in different combinations of the restaurant's ice-blue-and-black, and red-and-black color schemes walked briskly, delivering food from pass-through windows in front of the restaurant's two open kitchens on the right and left.

On one side near the pass-through, in a glass-enclosed cooking station, one of the cooks made a show of lighting the pan while preparing one of the restaurant's popular flambéed desserts.

In the glass-enclosed station on the opposite side of the restaurant, another cook chopped, sliced and diced vegetables at lightning speed. He twirled the knife as he finished preparing one of the restaurant's signature salads.

Artful 3D images of both cooks hovered up top near the ceiling.

Today, no one flagged him to a table for a conversation. Most of the high-profile patrons would show up for dinner, and he'd have to make the rounds then, acknowledging them.

Dominic spotted Bailey in a teal dress, having lunch at a four top with the businessman who'd flown in from New York. He gravitated in that direction.

Bailey saw him and flashed a smile that leaned more toward business than personal. "Here he is, Mr. Henshaw." She looked toward the middle-aged dark-haired man at the table. "Let me introduce you to my brother, Chef Dominic Crawford."

"Mr. Henshaw, it's a pleasure. My apologies for being late." Dominic shook hands with the businessman.

"It's a pleasure to meet you as well."

Bailey sat down and both men took their seats.

"How was lunch?" Dominic glanced over Bailey's half-empty plate with her usual order of a grilled pineapple-and-chicken salad.

From the potato tourne garnish still on the plate, Henshaw had ordered a ribeye.

"How was the steak?" Dominic asked.

"It was great." Henshaw gave an appreciative smile. "One of the best I've tasted. The seasoning was perfect."

A tall brunette server came by the table. As she cleared Bailey and Henshaw's plates, she glanced to Dominic. "Would you like me to bring you something, Chef?"

He really wasn't hungry, but a chef who didn't eat in his own restaurant was a bad sign.

Dominic looked to Henshaw and Bailey. "Have you decided on dessert yet?"

Bailey responded, "No, we haven't."

"Would you like me to bring an order of the flambé sampler?" the server asked.

That was exactly what Dominic had planned to suggest. "Please."

He made small talk with Henshaw and Bailey about flight delays, airports and the weather. As they conversed, the server returned with shooter glasses of peach cherry jubilee topped with fresh rum whipped cream, bananas Foster, and candied bacon and apples over vanilla ice cream.

Henshaw took a bite of the peach cherry jubilee and his brows shot up. "Wow. This takes me back. My grandmother had a peach orchard. She was a whiz when it came to making desserts with all of the fruit."

Dominic's thoughts took him on his own journey. Sitting on Philippa's porch, imagining what a house in the country might look like, he'd envisioned a garden. But a place with an orchard...

Bailey surreptitiously kicking his leg under the table brought him back.

She smiled at Henshaw. "Dominic definitely has some innovative ideas brewing."

Picking up on what he believed was the thread of the conversation, he added. "I do. Right now, my team and I are developing a farm-to-fork menu for an event."

"Oh, really?" Henshaw replied.

"Yes. We're striving to bring out those memories of home, like when you tasted the peach-cherry jubilee." Dominic leaned in. "When I was in Maryland…"

Dominic and Bailey said goodbye to Henshaw in the lobby of the restaurant.

As soon as the man walked out the door, Bailey looked to Dominic. "Can I talk to you please?"

Instead of heading for his upstairs office overlooking the dining room, she stalked into the nearby admin office used by the host staff.

As soon as he shut the door, she whirled around and faced him. "What was that?"

"What was what?"

"You talked for almost an hour about taste memories, orchards, houses in the country and cows. Oh, and bees?"

"You asked me to tell him about the ideas I had brewing."

"For Frost & Flame Atlanta. Not from your field trips in Nowheresville, Maryland."

"First of all, it's Bolan, Maryland. And second, hell yeah, my mind is in Maryland. I'm a week away from the *Shadow Valley* movie screening, but you pulled me out here for meetings. And maybe, if you wanted me to talk about brewing ideas the way you want me to, you should have let me get some sleep before you scheduled this meeting." Fatigue and frustration made him impervious to her patented death stare.

Bailey closed her eyes a moment and released a heavy breath. "If Mom and Dad didn't love you so much, I would trade you in for a better brother."

"You love me too much to get rid of me."

"I love my sensible brother who understands the value of investors, but he's not here. Seriously? Bees? Why?"

Maybe he had gone overboard, drawing out the whole ecosystem thing on a napkin. "We've been trying to tape a segment at a bee farm, but something always goes wrong, like yesterday. I ended up taking the morning and afternoon off."

"Really? You took time off? What did you do?"

From the look on her face, she might have already heard, and even if she hadn't, he wasn't going to lie about it. "I spent the time with Philippa."

"Philippa—that reminds me. I got a call from someone I know who works for one of the producers of *Best Chef Wins*. Destiny Mitchell pitched them an idea for a new show called *A Date with Destiny*. How a single girl goes from the heartbreak of being part of a love triangle to finding true love one meal at a time."

"Love triangle…" He was about to ask with who, but Bailey's face clued him in. "You mean me, her and Philippa."

"Ding, ding, ding. You win! And there's pictures and videos of the three of you at some dive bar to back up her claim. You're kissing Philippa and Destiny is confronting you about it before she stalks away."

"What? That didn't happen. Philippa and I were enjoying a night out with friends when Destiny showed up at the bar with her entourage. She hunted me down after you told her I was in Bolan. So far, Philippa hasn't called me about any issues with paparazzi or the press. But I should still warn her."

"Well, lucky for all of us, the latest Kardashian news cycle is on an upswing, and not very many people care about your little love triangle. It's already yesterday's news, at least until the reunion episode, where I'm sure Destiny will cry her eyes out to help pitch her new show."

"So, they're going ahead with the reunion show?"

"In one form or another. But that isn't your focus, and neither is Bolan. The screening party is done from a project perspective. You just have to execute it, and once you do, you're not ever going back. I need your eye on the ball that's important—Atlanta."

Dominic started to object about not ever going back to Bolan. But in the world of celebrity, long-distance relationships often had a short shelf life. But he also couldn't envision not seeing Philippa again.

For the next three days, Dominic stayed on task

with the restaurant and investor meetings, while brief conversations and texts with Philippa tided him over. But she was wearing down, carrying the load of the restaurant plus preparing for the screening party.

On the night before the event, they chatted by video as he sat on the couch and she lay in bed.

She yawned. "The trout and the rest of the vegetables came in today. So that's everything."

"Are Jeremy and Ben good on cutting the short ribs tomorrow?" Ben, a sous chef at Frost & Flame LA, had flown to Maryland that morning.

"Yep. They'll get it done." Philippa's eyelids drooped. "And..." She fell asleep.

There was no point in waking her.

He could end the call. But he stayed on, watching her sleep. Her nose wiggled with a soft, quiet snort, and he stifled a chuckle. She looked cute.

"Good night, Philippa," he whispered, tracing over her cheek on the screen.

The time where he could hold her in his arms again couldn't come fast enough.

Chapter Nineteen

Philippa stood in the viewing box at the indoor arena overlooking the dining area for the party. Nine hours ahead of the event that started at eight, the raised flooring, round tables, groupings of potted green plants and flowers provided hints of the coming transformation.

She turned and glanced behind her at the glass enclosed space.

Rachel had decorated the viewing box with a deep blue, U-shaped sectional, surrounding a large coffee table. Four tall bistro tables were also positioned along the side wall.

The adjoining bathrooms were clean, polished and stocked with artfully arranged baskets on the counter that possessed multiple convenience items including breath mints, deodorant and sewing kits.

Hopefully, the food service areas and all the staff would remain just as ready. She'd just completed a walk-through of the portable kitchens, making sure all the equipment worked, and pots, pans and utensils had been stocked, along with dishware. The only thing missing were disposable gloves.

In a couple of hours, Jeremy, Ben, Teale and a couple of kitchen workers would arrive at the portable kitchens to complete the advanced prep that hadn't already been done. Quinn was supervising normal operations at Pasture Lane through lunch. Once that ended at two, she'd oversee closing the restaurant with Bethany, and then both of them would come to the arena.

The only missing piece was Dominic. His last text message was to tell her he was on his way to the airport. By now, the private jet he was taking was already in the air.

"There you are." Zurie came into the viewing box. "I'm just checking in. How are things?"

"So far, so good."

Zurie glanced out the window. "Rachel may have her quirks, but she definitely knows what she's doing. I can't wait to see the finished product. And I can't wait to get my hands on the short ribs you guys are making tonight. When I sampled the test recipe, they were amazing," Zurie stage-whispered.

"Maybe you could send a few extra plates of that entrée to our table."

Philippa laughed. "I'll see what I can do."

While everyone at the party would receive the salad and dessert sampler plates, multiple entreés would be plated in smaller portions and brought to the table by servers on a tray. The servers would make at least three passes, giving the guests an opportunity to try different entrées or have a second or third portion of what they enjoyed.

Close to noon at Pasture Lane, as she supervised the packing of ingredients in a van and a refrigerated truck on the back dock, she glanced at her phone. Dominic's plane should have landed.

Later in the day, back in the kitchen, she checked on Quinn at the expeditor station and the lunch service.

"I'm going to the arena," Philippa said. "Call me if you need something."

"Okay, I will." Quinn stopped a server from picking up a plate in the window. Using a cloth, she wiped a spot of gravy off the rim as she spoke to the server. "Jackie's in the weeds. Can you help her out and take her order to table six? It's about to become a dead plate."

The server snagged the two orders and took them to the dining room.

Good call... Since their talk, Quinn seemed more focused, and her confidence had improved.

Philippa's phone buzzed in her pocket. It was a text from Dominic.

Running late. We're stuck in traffic.

But at least he's on his way. She answered.

No problem. We're good here. Can't wait to see you.

A moment later a GIF of the spaghetti scene from the movie *Lady and The Tramp*, appeared on her phone.

Philippa laughed and some of the tension lifted from her shoulders. Tonight was going to turn out great. She could feel it.

At the arena, Quinn walking into the portable trailer made Philippa stop seasoning the trout and look at the time. Where was Dominic?

She'd sent him a text, but he hadn't responded. He hadn't answered her calls either. Cell phone dead spots sometimes happened on the back roads to Tillbridge. If the driver had taken one as a short-cut, Dominic might not realize she was trying to contact him or be able to call. But if they were on a back road, that would mean Dominic was closer to getting there.

Moments later, the chime ringtone she'd recently programmed for Dominic played on her phone in her front pocket. Relief sang through her as she stripped off her disposable gloves to answer it. "Hi, are you almost here?"

"I'm still near Baltimore." The sound of passing traffic came through the phone.

"Are you stuck behind an accident?"

"No, but I was in one."

"What? Are you okay?"

Ben, searing short ribs nearby, glanced at her.

The wail of sirens on Dominic's end of the line fueled tingles of dread.

Swallowing panic, she left the kitchen trailer. "Dominic."

"I'm here."

"Are you okay? What happened?"

"My driver had a heart attack. One minute, he was driving, and the next, he slumped over the wheel."

"Oh, my..." Shocked, she stared at the two connected kitchen trailers just yards away. The ones Dominic would have been in if he were there. "Is he alright? What about you?"

"He's on his way to the hospital. I'm on my way there, too. I have a cut on my head. I need stitches."

Stitches? Dominic must have hit his head really hard. He could have a concussion. "Which hospital are you going to? I'll meet you." Philippa rushed toward the makeshift parking area where she'd left the golf cart.

"No, Philippa. You can't. The screening party. You have to stay there."

He was right. She couldn't leave. "I'll find someone who can pick you up."

"I'll call the car service. I need to make sure they know what happened, anyway. I'll ask them to send another driver to pick me up from the hospital."

"No. I'm finding someone."

A golf cart was coming across the field. It was Zurie.

Unable to stay put, Philippa started jogging toward her.

Zurie slowed to a stop beside her, concern on her face. "What's happened?"

Philippa filled her in.

"Let me talk to him." Zurie took the phone and got the pertinent details from him. "Got it. Just sit tight at the hospital. Someone will be there to get you. And you have my number? If anything changes, call me." She ended the call and gave Philippa her phone. "I'll call Mace. I'm sure he can pick him up."

"Thank you." Philippa's hand trembled as she put the phone in her pocket.

"Hey." Zurie reached out and squeezed Philippa's arm. "He's okay. He's on his way to the hospital. They'll take care of him, and Mace will get him here safely."

"I know. I should tell his team what happened. And mine."

"Take a minute before you do that. Let me call Mace, and then I'll come talk to you."

Philippa forced herself to breathe as she slowly walked back to the trailers, trying to envision what happened with Dominic and the driver. What *could* have happened.

I almost lost him... Her heart filled her throat.

A few deep breaths later, she rounded up Teale, Ben, Jeremy and Quinn and told them about Dominic's accident.

Teale grew pale. "He's going to the hospital, but he's okay, right?"

"As far as I know he just needs a few stitches."

Jeremy wrapped a protective arm around Teale's shoulders and whispered in her ear. Nodding, she leaned on him a moment, and then he let her go.

"What do you need us to do?" Jeremy asked.

"I'll need you and Teale to take over Dominic's two trailers. Quinn and Ben, I'll need you with me. You're all experienced supervisors, so I need you to take the lead with the cooks and kitchen staff that are working with us today and reassure them that we're still on track. Dominic and I picked you to work with us on this event because we knew we could count on you. And that's why I'm not worried. I know you'll do a fantastic job."

The group dispersed and walked to their assigned trailers.

Philippa took a moment to mentally lean into what she'd just told them. It wasn't lip service. Jeremy and Teale were in sync with each other and would easily take over Dominic's place. Ben was professional, precise and had good instincts about what had to be done, and Quinn was reliable and would also rise to the occasion. Having the four of them in place would allow her to oversee the entire food production process and keep an eye on quality control.

Anxious moments later, Zurie tracked her down. "Mace is on his way to Dominic."

"Good." Philippa released a pent-up breath. Knowing Dominic was taken care of and that he was counting on her, she focused.

As Philippa checked over the salads in one of the trailer's refrigerators, Eve showed up dressed to work.

"I heard about Dominic. What do you need me to do?"

Grateful to have another pair of experienced hands and Eve's eye for presentation, she assigned her to quality control and to keep things moving smoothly in the staging area set up in the corridor.

Time sped up as the start of the event grew closer. The atmosphere became even more intense when the party started and trays of food were taken from the trailers to the corridor.

Philippa settled into the calming space of what

she loved to do—create moments of solidarity for people with food. A moment where first bites ignited shared smiles and conversations. Where new taste memories were born and people would look back and say "Remember that meal?"

She made sure the honey-lemon dressing was drizzled just right over the salads. Monitored the cooking of the seared trout, making sure it was crispy and succulent as it rested on a twirl of veggie noodles. She ensured the glazed short ribs sat perfectly on creamy, Carolina Gold rice grits. That in the staging area, puffs of whipped cream sat like fluffy clouds on top of the fruit-based desserts.

As the last of the desserts left the table in the staging area, she closed her eyes and breathed. A happy high-pitched squeal made her open her eyes.

Rina hurried over to her, looking fabulous in a blue-green sleeveless jumpsuit and heels. "You killed it! Everything was beyond wonderful. I'm so proud of you." She briefly hugged Philippa, then leaned away. "And I have good news. Mace has Dominic. They're on the way. Dominic is fine."

"Thank you." Her whispered prayer came with an unexpected rush of latent adrenaline and relief. Happiness almost loosed tears.

Rina snatched a clean cloth napkin from the servers' backup stash on a table and put it in Philippa's hand. "No time for that. Dry your eyes. Wipe your face. And take off that apron. Holland Ainsley wants to acknowledge you onstage."

"But…"

"No *buts*. Come on." Rina tugged her down the corridor toward the front of the arena.

As they reached the hall archway leading to the arena, Philippa saw Dominic.

Her mind went blank to anyone or anything else as she ran to him. He took her in his arms.

His warmth and strength surrounded her, and she took in a shaky inhale, breathing him in. "Are you okay?" Not waiting for an answer, she cupped his cheek and kissed him. The firm press of Dominic's lips reassuring her that he was. Philippa leaned away and carefully skimmed over the bandage near his right temple.

"I'm fine." He smiled down at her. "They even did a scan at the hospital to make sure my head's okay. I just needed a few stitches, that's all."

Rachel came partway into the tunnel and smiled. "Dominic, you're okay."

"Yeah, I'm good."

Rachel beckoned. "Come on. Holland's waiting."

Philippa took Dominic's hand and stepped forward, but he didn't move. She looked back at him.

He smiled wider. "Not me. Just you."

She glanced to Rachel, who beckoned again. "Chef Gayle, come on. Holland's announcing your name."

* * *

Dominic nudged Philippa along, but she held on to him. "Go on." He kissed the back of her hand. "I'll be here when you're done. Promise."

Nodding, Philippa slipped her hand from his and followed Rachel.

A short time later, applause erupted, and pride swelled inside of him. Rachel had already told him how smooth everything had gone and that the attendees were raving about the food.

But he'd never worried or doubted her ability to handle the event without him. She'd been there for every step of the planning, and even made it easier for him. They shared the same vision, work ethic and level of passion. They made a good team.

Philippa came back to him with a happy grin on her face. "Wow. Did you hear that?"

"I did." He gave her a lingering kiss. "I'm really proud of you."

"Thank you, but I didn't do it on my own. Everyone helped. They heard what happened, and they really stepped up. I need to thank them. Are you coming? They were worried about you, especially Teale, Eve and Ben."

"No, I don't want the focus to be on me and what happened. I want you guys to celebrate the moment." His head throbbed, but he resisted touching the bandage. "I'm heading to your place. If that's alright."

Happiness flooded her face, and something tugged in his chest. "Of course it is. Do remember the codes for the door and the alarm?"

She refreshed his memory and hurried down the corridor to thank the staff.

As she walked away, some of the tension he'd carried since the accident left him.

Mace and Zurie came down the stairs from the viewing box and walked over to him.

Zurie looked around, then back to Dominic. "Where's Philippa? Did she see you?"

"She just went to thank everyone."

"I know she's glad you're okay," Zurie said. "We all are. I can't believe what happened."

"Neither can I. One minute, the driver, Pete, was talking about his grandkids, then the car started slowing down, and he slumped over. Seconds after that, we were rear-ended and spinning off the road."

Zurie's mouth dropped open. "It's amazing no one aside from the driver is in the hospital. That poor man."

Mace nodded. "I talked to one of the deputies on the scene. She said the driver taking his foot off the accelerator saved you both."

And Dominic was grateful for that. He'd felt so helpless in the back seat when Pete slumped over. The feeling had only grown during the seconds afterward, when he realized how much danger they were in with traffic speeding down the interstate around them.

Then the car had started to spin, but his mind had slowed, and Philippa's face came into his thoughts along with a sadness that he might not ever see her again.

Dominic breathed away the awful memory. "Any word on Pete's condition?" he asked Mace.

"Not yet. He's still in surgery. I can't get an update directly from the hospital, but the deputy said she'd call me once she heard something."

"And his family? Were they able to reach them?"

"They got a hold of his wife. She's at the hospital."

"Good." Pete had family with him. Hopefully, he would pull through.

Suddenly, a wave of soreness and tiredness hit Dominic and he massaged near his temple.

"Do want me to take you home?" Mace asked.

"If you do, you'll miss the start of the movie."

"She'll fill me in on what I missed later." Mace briefly kissed Zurie then turned back to Dominic. "Are you going to the cottage?"

"No." A longing to go where he wanted to be the most settled over him. "I'm going to Philippa's."

By the time Mace dropped Dominic off, his head was throbbing full force. After a long, hot shower, he found some pain reliever in the cabinet, took it, crawled into bed and immediately conked out.

A few hours later, the dipping of the mattress woke him up.

Slipping under the covers, Philippa glanced his direction. "Sorry, I didn't mean to wake you."

"That's okay. Come here. Let me hold you."

She snuggled close to him. The clean smell of soap-scented oil wafted from her. "I'm so glad you're okay."

"Me, too." There was so much more that he needed to tell her, but fatigue took hold of him again. One thought lingered as his eyelids closed. Holding Philippa in his arms felt like home.

The thought was still on his mind in the morning when he drifted into the kitchen.

Philippa, standing at the stove in a blue silky button-down sleep shirt, making eggs, was a beautiful sight. And one that he couldn't imagine not seeing again.

Dominic wrapped his arms around her from behind, and she leaned into him. He'd missed her so much when he'd been in LA. He didn't want to be apart from her again.

Reaching out, he turned off the burner under the skillet and turned her around by the waist to face him.

A surprised smile lit up her face. "What—?"

He kissed her hard and deep, savoring the sweep of his tongue over hers and the soft curves of her mouth.

Dominic eased away and stared into her eyes. "Come back with me to California. Before you say anything, hear me out. We're good together. And I don't want to miss a moment of being with you. I want to be there when you rise to the top—a bigger restaurant. A ton of cookbooks with your name on them. Your own show. And not just work. I want to share a home with you that tells the story of us. I want to build a life with you."

He'd meant to lay out his plan with more finesse, but the words had poured out of him.

"Oh, Dominic." An inner struggle played out in her eyes. As Philippa skimmed her fingers over the bandage on his head, her bottom lip trembled.

His heart started to sink. "Please, don't say no."

Soft emotions covered her face as she cupped his cheek. "I'm not saying no. I want all of those things with you. But I can't leave Tillbridge. At least not right away. I need some time. Five or six months, maybe. Is that okay with you?"

"Of course it is." Dominic held her close.

Every day they were apart, he'd wish for time to move faster to get her there. But in the end, they would be together, and that's what mattered.

Chapter Twenty

Philippa tidied her desk. Pasture Lane had closed after dinner over an hour ago. The staff were on their way out. She could finally go home to Dominic.

Home... It sounded so right to put that word and his name in the same sentence. But in a few months, home wouldn't be in Maryland. It would be in California with Dominic.

Two days had passed since she'd said yes, but she hadn't told anyone. She'd tried, but she couldn't say it. Maybe the uncertainty would go away if she wrote out her exit plan. One that would assure everyone that Pasture Lane would continue to thrive.

Leaving Rina would be even harder. Not that

they wouldn't remain friends. And since she wasn't leaving Maryland for at least six months, and Scott hadn't made the move from California yet, she and Rina could end up doing the long-distance-boyfriend commute together.

A vision of her and Rina, laughing on a plane bound for California came to mind. They would feed off each other's excitement, ready to see the guys they love.

But those trips wouldn't go on forever.

The image in her mind of her and Rina faded, and her optimism about the move went with it. Philippa shook it off. Expanding her career was a good thing. Being with Dominic was a wonderful thing. She was just experiencing a bit of anxiety over making a change.

The clang of oven racks being dropped on a metal table echoed into the office, and Philippa glanced out the window.

Jeremy wiped out the ovens on the other side of the kitchen.

That was strange. One of the kitchen helpers should have done that, and Jeremy was good about checking to make sure they did a good job. But he had been a little off the entire day.

Her phone rang. It was Dominic. He was probably wondering how much longer she would be. Philippa answered the call.

"Hey, I'm on my way out now. What about you?"

"We just wrapped up. I know you and I were planning to go straight home tonight, but apparently, I'm buying at the Montecito. Can you meet me there? We won't stay long."

"Sure. Can you give me twenty minutes or so?"

"That works. The crew is still packing up. I can swing by and get you."

Another loud clang from the kitchen drew her attention. "No. I'll meet you there. I need to talk to Jeremy."

"Everything okay?"

"I don't know. He's been quiet and moody. That's not like him."

"But it's understandable."

"Why?"

"Hold on a sec." During the pause, doors opened and shut on his end of the phone. "It isn't a secret, but Teale accepted a job offer. A designer luggage company is paying her to vlog her travels while cooking in places off the beaten path."

"Wow, that's exciting." More clanging reverberated from the kitchen. "But I'm guessing that means the end of her and Jeremy's relationship."

"Probably. I hate to lose her, too, for different reasons, obviously. They're not paying her much, and she's only guaranteed the position for six months, but this is her dream opportunity. She has to take it."

Years ago, Philippa had felt the same about going to Coral Cove for the interview audition. But honestly, despite everything that had happened with her and Dominic, if she was having a conversation with her twenty-two-year-old self, she wouldn't discourage her from taking healthy risks.

"She absolutely has to." Philippa turned off her computer. "I'm sure Jeremy understands, but that doesn't make it any easier for him."

"Or for Teale. Part of the reason why the team wants to go to the Montecito tonight is to cheer her up. She's really down about the breakup." Dominic released a long exhale. "I'm glad we were finally able to figure things out and that we're on our way to a new chapter."

"We are." Philippa waited for her own surge of gratefulness, but she wrestled with the same anxiety she'd felt a minute ago.

"A part of me thinks we should sit them down and tell them not to give up on each other."

A laugh slipped out of her. "You and I as relationship counselors? I don't know about that. We didn't exactly take the easy road to get here."

He chuckled softly. "Yeah, you're probably right. I have to go. Bailey's calling me on the other line. So I'll see you later?"

"Yes. I'll be there. Love you."

"Love you, too."

Love. The warmth Philippa felt in hearing and saying the important four-letter word wrapped around her heart like a hug. Yeah, anxiety on the verge of a huge shift like she was taking was absolutely normal. And what she and Dominic felt for each other would see her through it.

Philippa left her office. As the boss, it wasn't her place to pry into Jeremy's personal business, but she did need to address his earlier mood with the staff.

As she approached Jeremy, he glanced up from wiping out an oven on the other side of the table. "Hey, Chef."

"Hey. Are you heading out soon? It's been a long day."

"I just wanted to hit a few things I noticed. I'm off tomorrow, so staying late is no big deal."

"So, how do you think dinner service went tonight?"

"Things were slower than usual. And the line wasn't as focused as they should have been. They made a lot of mistakes."

"There was something I noticed that could have influenced what was happening on the line."

"Oh?" Jeremy paused.

"You seemed on edge."

"I did? I didn't mean to be. I guess I'm a little preoccupied." He picked up a metal rack from the table and slid it into the oven. "I don't know if you heard, but Teale is leaving Dominic's team."

"I heard she accepted a new position. It sounds like a great opportunity."

"Yeah, it is." He gave a lopsided grin. "She's going to have a great time traveling to all those places, meeting people, cooking, discovering all kinds of different ingredients and trying new stuff. Like she said, it's a dream job." He picked up a white kitchen towel from the table, staring down at it as he wiped his hands. "She asked me to go with her."

"She did?"

He looked up. "But of course I said no. I have a really nice apartment and a car I just paid off. And responsibilities. You're counting on me. And I like working here with you at Pasture Lane. I've learned a lot. I can't just walk away from everything. Sure, I've got some savings I could dip into, but what about when I get back? I could get another apartment, but there's no guarantee that you'd have a spot for me in six months. It's too risky."

Philippa caught the hint of conflict in his eyes. Who was he trying to convince? Her or himself?

Yes, she'd been counting on Jeremy to be there after she left Pasture Lane. But like she'd mentioned to Dominic, one of the things that she'd always wanted for Jeremy as her sous chef was for him to push himself a little harder.

Philippa joined Jeremy on the other side of the

table. "Set aside the risky part for a minute. Do you want to go? Would it make you happy?"

"Yes." Jeremy shrugged. "Obviously, I like Teale and want to be with her, but there's so much more to know about food and people and the recipes that are part of their culture. I could bring that back with me."

Dominic had said that what she saw in Jeremy, Chef LeBlanc had noticed in him. What was the advice he'd said she'd given him?

Philippa borrowed from it as she faced Jeremy. "Do you mind if I give you some advice?"

"No. I'm glad to get it."

"You can stay here and be comfortable, and that's perfectly okay. But don't let the risk of going with Teale scare you if going with her is something you really want to do, especially if you think you'll be happy doing it. Find someone to sublet your apartment. Let someone you trust take care of your car. And if it helps, your job will be here when you get back, if you still want it."

"You'll hold my job for me?"

"Yes." Jeremy getting his job back, she'd set that up with Zurie before she left. "With all the new knowledge you'll gain, it's nothing but a benefit to Pasture Lane if you come back and work for me. Think about it and let me know what you decide." She reached toward him and patted the table in a encouraging gesture. "I support you either way."

A pondering, more hopeful expression took over his face. "Okay. I'll think about it."

"Good." As she turned to walk away, a feeling of doing the right thing came over her.

"Chef Gayle."

She paused.

Jeremy gave a nod. "Thanks."

A half hour later, as Philippa pulled out of the parking lot at Tillbridge, Jeremy sped out ahead of her in his truck. Farther down the road, he turned left just like she planned to do, headed toward the Montecito.

If he was choosing to go with Teale, he was probably making the best choice and she was glad for him. She and everyone else would miss having him in the kitchen as a leader, but maybe this was the perfect opportunity to mentor Quinn and help her elevate her skills. The night of the movie screening, Quinn had really stepped up and impressed her. Gradually giving Quinn more responsibility while encouraging her to attend culinary workshops and other learning opportunities would help bring out her abilities even more.

As Philippa braked at the stop sign, then made the turn, reality swept in. She wouldn't be around to mentor Quinn. Someone else would have to do it. But would they see the same potential in her? And if Jeremy came back, what if the new head chef didn't encourage him to expand on what he'd learned traveling the world.

Worry, resignation and sadness bored down inside of Philippa. The letting-go process was hard. But it was worth it, right?

Set aside the risky part for a minute. Do you want to go? Would it make you happy?

Her advice to Jeremy still looped through her thoughts as she parked in the lot at the Montecito. She turned off the engine but remained in the car. Jeremy had said yes without hesitation, but when Dominic had presented his LA plan to her, she'd felt torn between wanting to be with him and remaining at Tillbridge. Jeremy had said he wanted to be with Teale…but the opportunity made him happy, too.

Did she feel the same way about the LA plan?

A knock on the window startled her out of her thoughts.

Dominic smiled, motioning she should unlock the door.

She did and he opened it.

As soon as she got out, Dominic shut the door behind her, then kissed her.

Philippa laid her hand to his chest as desire and bittersweetness swelled.

As if sensing it, he eased out of the kiss and leaned away. The parking lot lights illuminated the empathy on his face. "Are you sad about Jeremy? I saw him and Teale a minute ago. They're not telling everyone, but they told me that he's going with her. And he also mentioned how you're supporting him." Dominic cupped her cheek and tipped up her face. "You did a good thing. The right thing." He pressed his lips briefly to hers. "Come on. Let's go inside."

Dominic held her hand and took a step toward the Montecito.

"Wait." She tugged him back. "I can't go with you."

"Are you sure you don't want to come in? The team was looking forward to seeing you. We'll make it quick. Once I pay the bar tab, we can leave."

Sadness pushed in on Philippa's chest. She couldn't go inside and pretend that everything was okay. She had to tell him now. "No. I mean I can't leave Tillbridge and go with you to LA."

Dominic stood back in front of her. "I know you're worried about what will happen to Pasture Lane. If you have to stay on a few months longer to help everyone move past the transition without Jeremy, we'll figure it out." He gave her hand a squeeze. "I know it's hard to let go, but you can't let Jeremy leaving be the excuse that keeps you from moving on."

"It's not." As she let that sink in, the truth she'd been denying for the past two days emerged. "Being a part of your world has been exciting. But it's not me. Being here. Doing what I do at Tillbridge. It's enough for me."

"But what about us? Don't you want that?" As

he let go of her hand, he visibly swallowed. "I don't want a long-distance relationship with you."

"And I don't want that with you."

"Then, why are you playing small when you could have everything, including us being together?"

"Playing small?" She took a step back. "Is that what you think I've been doing here all these years?"

"I'm not saying what you achieved with Pasture Lane isn't important." Frustration leaped in his eyes. "But in LA, you would have a chance at other opportunities. That's all that I meant."

"Shows, cookbooks, a restaurant in a larger city—those things don't feel bigger to me. Leaving here and giving up my dreams would be playing small. I'm happy where I am. Are you?" The last comment hadn't been intended. It had just slipped out.

Dominic gave her a look, as if she'd shocked him by asking the question. Bleakness came into his eyes before he glanced away. When he met her gaze again, it was gone. "Are we really doing this?"

Ending their relationship in a restaurant parking lot? It was almost fitting. And it was like a cruel joke. Philippa took a shaky breath. "I think we are."

Dominic closed his eyes a moment. "Okay."

"Okay."

He started to walk away, but in three quick strides, he returned to Philippa and cupped her face. The hard press of his lips to hers stole her breath and broke her heart as she tasted the saltiness of tears.

In need of air, they broke apart. Breathing hard, he laid his forehead to hers. "I have to go."

Hands tucked in his front pockets, he stalked toward the Montecito.

Tears blurred her eyes as she got back in the car and watched him go inside. Philippa swiped them from her face, started the car and drove out of the parking lot.

Before she realized it, she was pulling into Rina's driveway. She turned off the engine.

Scott walked out of the house and onto the brightly lit porch. As he glanced back, Rina came out, comfortable for the night in shorts and T-shirt.

Philippa gripped the keys still in the ignition. She was intruding. She should go.

But as Rina came closer, Philippa got out.

Rina paused and stared at her. "Oh no. What's wrong?"

"Dominic and I, we… I…" Philippa couldn't even say it.

"Oh, honey." Rina rushed over and hugged her. "I got you. It's okay." She rocked Philippa like a child, then put an arm around Philippa's shoulders and guided her to the house.

They sat on the couch in the living room.

Philippa's eyes felt gritty and tight, but there

were no more tears. They were trapped in the icy ball of disbelief lodged in her chest. "I shouldn't have interrupted you and Scott."

"Don't worry about that." Rina grabbed hold of Philippa's hand. "What happened?"

Philippa took a deep breath and poured out her heart.

Chapter Twenty-One

Dominic walked into his upstairs office at Frost & Flame, grateful the dinner meeting downstairs with him, Bailey and the latest potential investor she'd found for Frost & Flame Atlanta was over. It was their third meeting that week, each of them beginning to feel like a command performance where he hyped his vision, and she backed him up with a set of impressive numbers.

He took off his blue suit blazer and laid it over the arm of the black leather sofa. As he unbuttoned and rolled up the sleeves of his crisp white dress shirt, he glanced at his desk. A full in-box waited for him. He was going to be there awhile.

But instead of sitting down, he stuck his hands

in his front pockets and stared out the dark tinted window overlooking the dining room. But in its place, he saw Pasture Lane's kitchen in his mind. And Philippa. He longed to hold her. And to change how things had ended between them two weeks ago.

Then, why are you playing small when you could have everything?

A part of him had known he'd messed up when he said it, but he'd been frustrated and hurt that she'd changed her mind about joining forces with him and building a life together. All he could think about was that she was pushing him away again, like she had before she'd left Coral Cove.

No. Leaving here and giving up my dreams would be playing small. I'm happy where I am. Are you?"

Her question in the Montecito parking lot lingered in his mind.

Was he happy about losing her again? He wasn't. But Philippa claimed she was happy at Pasture Lane. And he had responsibilities that demanded his full attention. There was no point in stretching out the inevitable with a long-distance relationship. They not only lived on opposite coasts, but they were also moving in different directions.

The door to his office opened and closed.

In the reflection of the window, he watched Bailey walk toward him looking like she owned the world in a scarlet business suit.

She stood beside him. "Russ is on his way to the airport. I think he'll still be raving over the rib-eye steak he had for dinner when he gets back to New York."

"I'm glad he enjoyed it." He looked to Bailey. "So?"

The one-word question encapsulated what was on both their minds. Did they have a new investor?

She crossed her arms over her chest. "He didn't say no. But he didn't say yes either. Honestly, I give him until he lands to give us his answer. No."

"But you just said he was raving about the food. And he seemed impressed by the numbers."

"Yes, Russ was impressed by all of that. But what he wasn't impressed with was you."

"He said that?"

"He didn't have to. I could see it on his face, just like I could with the other two potential investors when you were talking about the future of the restaurant. Hell. I wasn't even impressed."

"Not impressed?" Irritation poured heat into his face and out of the collar of his open shirt. "I didn't talk about farm-to-fork concepts, so that can't be the problem. Let me guess. I didn't smile or laugh in all the right places?"

"Actually, you did. Like I'd given you a script. You're not feeling it, and we can all tell."

"All? You make it sound like there's a hoard of people in on this."

"Well, let's see..." Bailey counted off on her fingers. "There's Eve, Brianne and the rest of the production crew for your show. And the entire restaurant staff, they're totally confused. I heard you haven't cooked in the restaurant for over a week and barely come downstairs to greet the VIPs or the rest of the customers."

"Because I'm busy." He jabbed his finger in the air toward his desk. "I've got a full load of work waiting for me, or hasn't anyone noticed?"

"You've been twice as busy, and it never affected your performance before. You have to face—"

"Don't say it. You're about to bring Tillbridge into the conversation, and I don't want to hear it. I don't want to be here all night." Dominic went to his desk. "You mentioned earlier you left papers for me to sign."

Bailey slammed her palm down on the stack in his in-box. "Screw the papers. And this isn't just about Tillbridge."

Her eyes growing bright as if they were about to well with tears cooled his anger. Bailey never cried. Not even when they were kids and she fell off her bike, skinning both of her knees.

He walked over to her. "Bailey, what's wrong?"

Laying her hand to her stomach, she took a breath, quickly recomposing herself. "You're not listening. The problem is you. You haven't been yourself for a while. I thought you were tired or on the edge of burnout, so that's why I got you the contract for the screening party."

"Got me the contract? You said Holland requested me."

"She was perfectly content with what Tillbridge had to offer, but she went along with the change as a favor to me. And then I used every bargaining chip I had to get the production company to kick in the budget for you to tape your farm-to-fork episodes there. I thought running around the countryside would re-inspire you."

She'd sent him to Tillbridge? He turned away from her a moment as he ran his hand across his nape. "So when I asked you to get me out of the contract and you wouldn't, it had nothing to do with money or my image?"

"No."

"And Philippa? How did she fit into your plan?"

"She didn't. I found out that she was the chef at the property the same day the contract arrived for you to sign. I'd hoped that she was far enough in your rearview that it wouldn't matter. If anything, I thought seeing her would remind you of how much you'd enjoyed your sous chef days at Coral Cove, and those memories might inspire you, too. I was just trying to do the right thing."

He couldn't be mad at her for that. Bailey was a handful, but she also truly cared about him.

Dominic pulled her in for a mutual one-armed

hug. "You could have just told me to take a vacation."

Bailey playfully pushed him away. "Like you would have listened to me." Her small smile faded as sincerity came into her eyes. "But you have to listen to me now. Go away for a few days. Unplug. Work things out in your head. Figure out your future. Sleep. Do whatever it is you want to do. Then come back recharged. We need you. I need you."

He had felt more worn down than usual since returning from Maryland. A chance to get away from it all sounded great. "But we have episodes to shoot for the show and meetings lined up. And we still haven't found someone to replace Teale."

"Piece of cake. I'll handle it. Really, I've got this." She patted his arm. "Just go."

Dominic walked out the back door onto the porch of the beach bungalow, carrying a bowl of cubed, fresh mango. As he sat on the lower step in his blue-and-white swim shorts, warm white sand caved around his bare feet. An afternoon breeze filled with ocean brine whispered over him.

He'd slept past noon. It had taken three days for his body to adjust and not automatically wake him up before dawn with his schedule running through his mind. Bailey had been right. He'd needed this.

After polishing off the mango, he set the bowl on the step and walked the beach. The private island, owned by a friend of a friend, wasn't Coral Cove, but the palm and cassia trees landscaped into the front of the bungalow had stirred up the good memories of being there as a sous chef. The sumptuous meals he'd cooked for the guests. The skills he'd learned from Chef LeBlanc. Supervising the staff. The place he'd shared with five other people in Bridgetown that was basically a shack. Those experiences had launched him to where he was now.

Lured by the rise and fall of the glittering ocean, he went into it, diving in where the sand dropped off and the water grew deep. Sometime later, he swam in on the gentle push of a wave, and as he walked back up on the beach, a peacefulness reminiscent of being at Coral Cove washed over him. He'd had responsibilities back then, but inside he'd been carefree.

But he'd felt it before...with Philippa.

He imagined seeing the two of them walking in the surf, laughing, kicking up water and chasing each other. Her laughing as he carried her into the waves. But what he saw was from six years ago. The Philippa he knew back then belonged on the beach in his memories. The woman he knew now was right where she was supposed to be, in the countryside, under the bright blue sky and the radiance of the sun. She was in the kitchen at Pasture Lane, sharing the food she loved and mentoring her staff. And more importantly, she knew that was where she belonged.

As far as himself... The guy who'd walked the beaches of Coral Cove with Philippa no longer existed, either. And as good as it had been for him, he had no desire to rewind the clock and go back in time to the island resort. But he wanted to feel that sense of lightness in his heart and soul and the purpose he'd once felt. He'd lost that along the way. And found it with Philippa.

I'm happy... Are you?

Two days later, as the sun started to dip low into the ocean, he held his phone in his hand. It had remained off since he'd been there, but he had an important call to make.

Bailey thought she needed him, but she didn't. And now it was time for her to rise and take over what she'd put her time and heart in to build. His restaurant enterprise. She'd still have his name and his support, but the vision would be hers, not his.

He dialed her number.

She picked up on the third ring. "Hi." Bailey's tone was light almost playful. "Love you. But I'm hanging up unless it's an emergency. You're on vacation."

"It's not an emergency, but..."

Bailey hung up.

A chuckle huffed out of him. He'd walked into that one. Dominic called her again.

She answered, and he jumped right in. "Hang up again, and I'm sending someone to your house to take all your favorite stuff, including the stash of peanut-butter-cup ice cream."

"My ice cream? Wow. You don't have to take it that far. I'm listening."

The importance of his decision and big-brother protectiveness made him pause. No, he wasn't abandoning her. Bailey really didn't need him. She needed him to step out of her way.

Dominic smiled as he watched the sun, slip farther below the horizon. "I've worked out my future..."

Chapter Twenty-Two

Philippa reversed the golf cart out of a space in the parking lot of the guesthouse. At six in the morning, only three people were in the lot—a couple, packing their bags into an SUV, and a man who had jogged to his car, grabbed something from the front of it, and was now jogging back to the guesthouse.

Tristan had called her last night and asked her to come to the indoor arena. Tillbridge was planning some sort of event there next month that would require food.

As she sped down the narrow-paved trail, she recalled riding to the arena a few weeks ago with Tristan for the meeting with Rachel...and seeing Dominic there. On that day, frustration and confusion had almost kept them apart, but what they felt for each other had allowed them to figure it out, to listen and talk. And find their way back to each other.

But what if she'd known then that they wouldn't make it? Would she have chosen for them to just remain friends? It would have been safer that way, but then she would have missed out on the good moments they'd shared while he was there. Like when they'd told each other "I love you" on the dance floor at the Montecito.

Reconciling the good with the bad of what happened between her and Dominic was something she was learning to do. Hopefully with time, it would become easier.

Using the updated code Tristan had given her, she entered he field through the pasture gate, then drove to the arena. Another golf cart was in the parking lot.

Tristan was already there.

Inside the building, she walked through the dark wood lobby and out the door near the reception desk leading to the main part of the arena.

Glimpsing Tristan standing in the viewing box, she veered right, then up the stairs to get there.

The door was already open and she walked inside. "Good morning, Tristan."

"Hey Philippa." He glanced up from typing a message on his phone and smiled. "Thanks again for meeting me."

"No problem. So what is this event again? I didn't see it on the schedule."

"It just came up and it's not booked yet. Right now, I'm just trying to get a feel on if we should agree to do it. It would take place out back. We'd have to use trailers again, like we did with the screening party. Let's head back there. I need a visual reference."

They left the viewing box and she walked with him down the wide corridor. "Can you give me an idea about the menu? The type of food they want will determine the setup."

His phone rang and Tristan glanced at the screen. "I should take this." He answered. "Hey, Rick. Yep... Nope... I know you need her back. Yes, I fed her..."

Was that one of the stable's boarding clients? If they were that worried, they must have been new to Tillbridge. The staff at the stable took great care of the horses.

Tristan glanced at Philippa as he continued to talk. "You're fifteen minutes out? I'll see if I can speed things up. Hold on a sec." He paused and waved Philippa forward. "Go on ahead. You can get a jump on things. I'll meet you out there."

"Okay." Philippa kept walking. A jump on what? He still hadn't told her about the event or the menu.

As she approached the back door, the sound of moo-ing cows floated through the corridor.

She was hearing things. Tristan would have mentioned cows.

But she heard the sound again. Philippa cautiously pushed open the door and peeked outside.

A dairy cow standing in a portable corral mooed at her.

Confusion made her open the door wider.

Close to the corral, a small tree in a black pot sat next to a round cafe table. On top of the table was a basket filled with fresh carrots, red peppers and tomatoes.

Movement to the left drew her attention, and her breath caught in her chest. It was Dominic.

A smile shadowed his lips. "Hello, Philippa." He looked good, a bit thinner but rested.

Just as she was about to ask him why he was there, a plausible answer came to mind. Was he part of the event Tristan was talking about? Tristan had mentioned wanting to get a feel on if they should agree to do it. Maybe this meeting was really about determining if she and Dominic could still work together.

If that was the case, she could handle it. Catering events at Tillbridge was her responsibility, and this was about professionalism. Not her feelings. She and Dominic made a good team in the kitchen.

They just weren't destined to have a personal relationship.

A dull ache swelled in her chest. Her mind accepted the truth, now she just had to make her heart understand.

As Dominic approached her, she quelled her mixed emotions and schooled her face. "Tristan had to take a call. He'll be here in a minute." She shifted her attention from him to the cow. "He mentioned an event, but he didn't give me any details about it. I'm assuming it's a farm-to-fork theme like we created for the screening event?"

"No. It's about hoping you'll forgive me."

"What?" Philippa looked up at him. Clearly she was hearing things. "Can you repeat that?"

As he stepped closer, sincerity filled his gaze. "I'm sorry. I'm sorry for what I said to you before I left. And I'm sorry that I hurt you instead of facing the truth about my life. You asked me if I was happy where I was. I wasn't. I thought the solution was for you to move to California so we could be together, but by asking you to do that, I was limiting your happiness. I was the one who needed to make a change. Not you."

Hope intensified, but as Philippa glanced at the cow and the table, she grew confused. "What are you trying to tell me. And what's all of this?"

"This is what I want."

"So you want...cows?"

He laughed. "Cows, chickens, and maybe even a goat grazing next to a house with a big kitchen, and a garden in the backyard. Or even an orchard."

The enthusiasm in his voice made Philippa see it in her mind. "But what about your restaurants and your show?"

"I'm grateful for Frost & Flame and *Dinner with Dominic*, but it's time for me to move on to what I really want. And I want it with you." He cupped her cheek, but a huge welt on his wrist stole her attention.

She grasped his hand and took it from her cheek. "Oh my gosh, Dominic. What happened?"

"The bees at the bee farm. I guess the owner was right about them not being happy. At least not with me. I went there yesterday to get honey to put in the basket, and this bee flew out of nowhere and stung me. But it's all good. The staff at the farm shot me up with an EpiPen, and then Tristan took me to the emergency room."

"Emergency room?" Concern raised her voice an octave.

"I'm fine, now. I'm slightly allergic to bee venom."

"Cross-cultivating bees is definitely off the list of things we'll be doing at the farm slash orchard."

"So is that a yes to us getting back together?"

It had taken six years for Dominic to come back into her life, and Philippa couldn't imagine another day without him. "It is."

Dominic slipped his arms around her, and the joy growing inside of her reflected on his face.

As they met halfway for a kiss, the potent smell of manure wafted in the air.

He glanced at the cow and grimaced. "Whoa. That's strong. Maybe we'll skip the cows and just visit Lula at Rick's farm."

Philippa laughed. Her city guy had a lot to learn about living in the country. "Deal. No bees. No cows. And no gardening in the dark with a family of raccoons."

"What?"

"Never mind." A truck with a livestock trailer driving through the pasture caught her attention. "I think it's time for Lula to go home."

As she went to move away, Dominic held her in place. "I love you."

Philippa stared up at him, and what had lived in her heart from the first moment she'd looked into his cinnamon-colored eyes filled her heart. "I love you, too."

Chapter Twenty-Three

Two years later...

Philippa unwrapped the corn on the cob in the foil. Steam filled with savory goodness rose from the lightly charred, golden kernels. She flashed a smile at the cameras in the studio kitchen in the cottage at Tillbridge. "Chili lime corn on the cob. The perfect addition to your next barbecue."

Dominic stood beside her. "Sweet and spicy. Just the way I like it," he murmured.

She glanced at him, and he stared at her instead of at the camera or the dish they'd just made. Passion and heat flashed in his eyes and her breath hitched.

"Cut. That's a wrap," Brianne said.

Dominic swooped in for a kiss and Philippa leaned into him.

"Alright, you two. Get a room." Brianne smiled as she called out to them from near one of the cameras.

Chuckling, Dominic's lips drifted toward Philippa's ear. "That's not a bad idea."

"I agree. After the late nights we've been putting in. I could use a nap." Smiling, Philippa laid her hand to the middle of Dominic's chest as he cupped her waist. "But someone's waiting for us."

Philippa looked beyond the cameras, and he followed her gaze.

Tristan stood at the opening of the hallway.

Dominic gave her a squeeze and kissed her cheek. "Go ahead. I need to talk to Brianne about the segment we're shooting tomorrow."

Drawn like a magnet, Philippa went to Tristan, who held a baby close to his chest. "Look, Angel." He pointed to Philippa. "Your mama's here."

Philippa's heart swelled as Angelique Renee Crawford cooed and smiled at her. "Hi, sweetie." She took the now-squirming baby in her arms and held her near her shoulder. "Thanks for watching her on such short notice."

The young woman who usually watched Angelique on set, in the nursery outfitted in the cottage's main bedroom, had fallen ill with a cold.

"No problem. I enjoyed it." Tristan transferred a small towel from his shoulder to Philippa's. "She ate not too long ago, and I changed her diaper."

Dominic walked up beside them. "How's my girl?" As he talked to her, Angelique stared at her daddy and he stared back, both enthralled with each other.

Philippa completely understood the sentiment. Some days she woke up, thought about her life now and almost had to pinch herself because it was so wonderful. A large part of that happiness came from being with Dominic, and now, Angelique.

Since their small wedding at Tillbridge a little over a year and half ago with their family and friends in attendance, Dominic had completely stepped away from the day-to-day running of Frost & Flame LA and Frost & Flame Atlanta. Head chefs oversaw the establishments, and Bailey managed the entire restaurant enterprise and any projects associated with them.

Dominic also had a new show, *Farm to Fork with Dominic Crawford.* Just like he dropped in from time to time to cook at Pasture Lane, she sometimes appeared as a guest on the show. He was taping at the cottage until he could move into the studio kitchen attached to their dream home that was being built. They were located a short distance from Rina and Scott.

"I better get back to the stable," Tristan said.

"Are you two still coming to the house for dinner tonight? Chloe's been texting me all morning from the set in Canada. She can't wait to get back here, especially to see Angelique."

"We'll be there." Laughing, Philippa gave into Angelique reaching for her dad and handed her to Dominic. "Should we bring anything besides this little handful?"

"Nope. Rina and Scott are helping out. Just show up around seven."

A couple of hours later, back at the house they were renting in Bolan, Philippa tiptoed out of the nursery where Angelique slept.

As she shut the door behind her, Dominic embraced her from behind.

She leaned into him. "Hey, we have some time before dinner at Tristan and Chloe's. We can test that brussels sprout recipe you were interested in."

"We could." He kissed her earlobe, and the warmth of his mouth radiated over her cheek. "Or we can take that nice, long nap you mentioned… among other things."

"But we really should get ahead on…" Words slipped away as Dominic trailed his lips down the side of her throat and slid his hand under her shirt.

"You were saying?" he murmured.

His palm gliding along her belly and moving upward erased the rest from her mind. He still possessed the ability to easily distract her.

Philippa turned in Dominic's arms and faced him. "I was saying that you're right."

In one smooth movement, he leaned down and swept her up in his arms.

As she looped her hands around his neck, she suppressed a squeak to a quiet laugh. "What are you doing?"

He carried her down the hall to their bedroom. "Not wasting a minute of my time with you."

In bed, as they lay in each other's arms. Dominic's deep kisses and caresses made her heart pound faster. She arched up her hips, hoping to coax him to where she needed him most. "Please…"

He gave her what she wanted, gliding inside of her, but then he paused, staring into her eyes. "How did I get so lucky?"

Philippa cupped his cheek, seeing their journey from Coral Cove to now. She knew the answer. "It wasn't luck. It was love."

* * * * *

For more second chance romances,
check out these great stories:

The Single Mom's Second Chance
By Kathy Douglass

The Father of Her Sons
By Christine Rimmer

The Most Eligible Cowboy
By Melissa Senate

Available now wherever
Harlequin Special Edition books
and ebooks are sold!

WE HOPE YOU ENJOYED
THIS BOOK FROM

◆HARLEQUIN
SPECIAL
EDITION

Believe in love. Overcome obstacles. Find happiness.

Relate to finding comfort and strength in the
support of loved ones and enjoy the journey
no matter what life throws your way.

6 NEW BOOKS AVAILABLE EVERY MONTH!

HSEHALO2020

COMING NEXT MONTH FROM

Ⓗ HARLEQUIN
SPECIAL EDITION

#2887 A SOLDIER'S DARE
The Fortunes of Texas: The Wedding Gift • by Jo McNally
When Jack Radcliffe dares Belle Fortune to kiss him at the Hotel Fortune's Valentine's Ball, he thinks he's just having fun. She's interested in someone else. But from the moment their lips touch, the ex-military man is in trouble. The woman he shouldn't want challenges him to confront his painful past—and face his future head-on...

#2888 HER WYOMING VALENTINE WISH
Return to the Double C • by Allison Leigh
When Delia Templeton is tapped to run her wealthy grandmother's new charitable foundation, she finds herself dealing with Mac Jeffries, the stranger who gave her a bracing New Year's kiss. Working together gives Delia and Mac ample opportunity to butt heads...and revisit that first kiss as Valentine's Day fast approaches...

#2889 STARLIGHT AND THE SINGLE DAD
Welcome to Starlight • by Michelle Major
Relocating to the Cascade Mountains is the first step in Tessa Reynolds's plan to reinvent herself. Former military pilot Carson Campbell sees the bold and beautiful redhead only wreaking havoc with his own plan to be the father his young daughter needs. As her feelings for Carson deepen, Tessa finally knows who she wants to be—the woman who walks off with Carson's heart...

#2890 THE SHOE DIARIES
The Friendship Chronicles • by Darby Baham
From the outside, Reagan "Rae" Doucet has it all: a coveted career in Washington, DC, a tight circle of friends and a shoe closet to die for. When one of her crew falls ill, however, Rae is done playing it safe. The talented but unfulfilled writer makes a "risk list" to revamp her life. But forgiving her ex, Jake Saunders, might be one risk too many...

#2891 THE FIVE-DAY REUNION
Once Upon a Wedding • by Mona Shroff
Law student Anita Virani hasn't seen her ex-husband since the divorce. Now she's agreed to pretend she's still married to Nikhil until his sister's wedding celebrations are over—because her former mother-in-law neglected to tell her family of their split!

#2892 THE MARINE'S RELUCTANT RETURN
The Stirling Ranch • by Sabrina York
She'd been the girl he'd always loved—until she married his best friend. Now Crystal Stoker was a widowed single mom and Luke Stirling was trying his best to avoid her. That was proving impossible in their small town. The injured marine was just looking for a little peace and quiet, not expecting any second chances, especially ones he didn't dare accept.

YOU CAN FIND MORE INFORMATION ON UPCOMING HARLEQUIN TITLES, FREE EXCERPTS AND MORE AT HARLEQUIN.COM.

HSECNM0122A

SPECIAL EXCERPT FROM

HARLEQUIN
SPECIAL EDITION

*From the outside, Reagan "Rae" Doucet has it all:
a coveted career in Washington, DC, a tight circle of
friends and a shoe closet to die for. When one of her
crew falls ill, however, Rae is done playing it safe.
The talented but unfulfilled writer makes a "risk list"
to revamp her life. But forgiving her ex, Jake Saunders,
might be one risk too many...*

*Read on for a sneak peek of
Darby Baham's debut novel,*
The Shoe Diaries, *the first book in*
The Friendship Chronicles *miniseries!*

"I won! I won!"

"That you did," he said, laughing and trying to climb
out of his own tube. With his long legs, he was having
a hard time getting out on his own, so I reached out my
hand to help him up. As soon as he grabbed me, we both
went soaring, feet away from the slides. I was amazed
neither of us fell onto the ground, but I think just when
we were about to, he caught me midair and steadied us.

"Okay, so a deal is a deal. Truth. Do you like me?"

"I can't believe you wasted your truth on something
you already know."

"Maybe a girl needs to hear it sometimes."

"Reagan Doucet, I will tell you all day long how much
I like you," he said, bending down again so he could

stare directly into my eyes. "But you have to believe me when I do. No more of that 'c'mon, Jake' stuff. You either believe me or you don't."

"Deal," I said, grabbing hold of the loops on the waist of his pants to bring him even closer to me. "You got it."

"Mmm, no. I've got you," he whispered, bringing his lips centimeters away from mine but refusing to kiss me. Instead, he stood there, making me wait, and then flicked out his tongue with a grin, barely scraping the skin on my lips. It was clear Jake wanted me to want him. Better yet, crave him. And while I could also tell this was him putting on his charm armor again, I didn't care. I was in shoe, Christmas lights and sexy guy heaven, and for once I was determined to enjoy it. Not much could top that.

"Now, let's go find these pandas."

I reached out my hand, and he took it as we went skipping to the next exhibit.

Don't miss The Shoe Diaries *by Darby Baham,*
available February 2022 wherever
Harlequin Special Edition books and ebooks are sold.

Harlequin.com

HSEEXP0122A